North Avenue

BY

Brendan Brogan

Dedication

This book is dedicated to St. Kathy,
who has been on special assignment
for over forty years as
my wife.
She is the heart of our family, raising
her three children and six
grandchildren.
They don't come any better!

&

To all the characters in this story who
Inspired me to write *North Avenue*.

Special Dedication in Memoriam

To Bob Arnold, one of my dearest and
closest friend, far from the womanizer he portrays
in this story. Bob was one of the good guys and is
now in Heaven with Buzz.

Brendan Brogan
July 27, 2003

NORTH AVENUE IS A WORK OF FICTION.
ALL EVENTS ARE FICTIONAL.

PRINTED IN THE USA.

edited by
Cece Whittaker
Easton One Productions
1-800-367-9551
www.editandco.com

printed by
Central Plains Book Manufacturers
Winfield, KS
August, 2003

Chapter One
Airport

Fitz Beckley adjusted the lapel on her Evan Picone blazer. Experience told her that timing was everything. She had set the perfect internal pace. Her standards were rigid on the inside. But outwardly, she sat casually, sipping a glass of white wine, flanked on either side by foreign men.

"I like this place," said the larger man, known in his profession as "Train." He was an enormous man in his middle forties who spoke with an imposing accent. "What do you call it?"

His companion chuckled. "Houllihan's," he answered. "It's new to you, is it, Eric?"

"You can call me Eric in public," snapped the larger man.

"Forget public," Fitz cut in. "You two may have time to kibbutz but I'm here on business."

"She told *you*, Tim," the Train said, a hint on condescension in his voice.

"Have another glass of wine," Tim urged Fitz. "We're going to have more beer."

"You two drink beer as if it were water," Fitz shot back. "And no, I think I've had quite enough."

"In our country, it is our water!" the Train said. He reached a hand fully around the base of the mug the bartender set before him. "To water!" He raised the mug.

Tim raised his mug in response. His bulk was nearly as remarkable as his cohort's. He stood slightly shorter at six-foot-two, but carried the same staunch build, as well as many scars from the rigors of his profession.

Fitz scowled and sighed. "This operation is very important to my organization," she began. "I take a dim view of mendaciousness."

Tim leaned back on his barstool and caught the Train's eye. "What's *mendaciousness*?" he mouthed.

The Train shrugged and shook his head.

"We understand," said Tim. "We respect your feelings on mentality."

The Train turned away, appearing to cough.

Fitz rolled her eyes. "Let me have the number," she barked.

When she had received the phone number to Tim's cellular phone, she tested it. Satisfied that it was correct when, indeed, it rang, the three began to go over the details of the operation that was set to occur later that day.

"Flight 17, Flight 17," an overhead speaker beaconed, "all passengers for Flight 17 please proceed to Gate Twelve. Please have your boarding passes ready…"

At 3:30 pm, Fitz departed Houlihan's. Her destination was Delta Airlines, Gate Eleven, on Concourse A.

"Excuse me, ma'am," she said at the boarding counter. "Can you tell me if flight 515 from Hartford is on time?"

"Yes indeed!" the perky woman responded. "Due to land in six minutes. Passengers will arrive in about twenty. Please make yourself comfortable. Have a seat."

"Thank you," said Fitz. It was only then that she allowed her guard to drop for a few moments. Forty-three years of walking on the hospital floor, albeit in sensible nurses shoes, had taken a toll on her feet. She was ready for a breather.

She selected a spot with a keen view of the ramp, down which departing passengers would travel. Checking her watch, she sat back and waited.

"Now arriving, Flight 515 from Hartford, Connecticut!" announced the bubbly attendant. "Passengers will disembark in about ten minutes."

Fitz extracted the newspaper she carried in her bag. She adjusted it carefully so as see without being seen by anyone alighting Flight 515 or the surrounding area. Her body was rock steady, but her nerves were raw. This was her first assignment, even though she had been with the organization for two years.

"Don't screw it up, Fitz," she muttered under her breath.

Just then, three suits arrived in dark glasses, one carrying a brief case. Approaching officiously, footsteps sharp, and clearly led by a tall, fit, middle-aged black man, they approached Perky. The leader was followed by two younger, trim, white associates, who appeared to be freshly graduated from the academy.

Fitz leaned forward, attempting to eavesdrop on the conversation. She had recognized them immediately. Their paths had crossed less than twenty-four hours earlier.

"Who's in charge here?" the leader asked in a commanding but not impolite tone.

The attendant, for once, changed expression. Wide-eyed, she answered, "Well, Mr. Cronin. He…"

"Please have him join us," the leader interrupted. "Immediately."

Perky disappeared behind a door.

The tall man, Marvin Lemons, turned to his associates and nodded. They casually approached, eyes darting continuously about the airport.

Before long, a pudgy fellow with a bright red jacket approached the men. He carried with him a clipboard and on his waist was attached a two-way radio. Extending his hand, he said, "Hello, I'm Charles Cronin with Delta Airlines. What can I do for you?"

Marvin shook his hand briefly. "Mr. Cronin, I am Marvin Lemons. This is Mr. Jenkins and Mr. Thomas." The other two moved up quickly, shook the man's hand, and rapidly retreated, all the while scanning the area, never once making eye contact.

Mr. Cronin's heartbeat increased. "Is there a problem?"

He did not think to ask Mr. Lemons for any identification at that point. But if he had, Lemons could have produced his shield, which had rested in his wallet for over forty years.

"Do you have a passenger on Flight 515 from Hartford, Connecticut by the name of Charles Downham?" Lemons asked.

"Let me check," Cronin answered. He consulted his clipboard. "No," he said, rubbing his forehead. "I don't see a Downham listed on this flight. I could check…"

"Excuse me," Lemons cut in. He stepped away and spoke quickly to Mr. Jenkins, who then removed himself from the group by about ten paces. He retrieved his cellular phone, made a brief call, and spoke in a huddle with Mr. Lemons.

Lemons approached Cronin. "He sometimes travels under the alias Mike Nixon," he advised. "Can you please check for that name?"

Cronin busied himself in his list. Momentarily his head rose triumphantly. "Yes! We have a Mike Nixon in row 22, seat B!"

"All right, Mr. Cronin," said Lemons in a low voice, "please listen carefully. We need Mr. Nixon urgently to participate in a critical conference call between the Pentagon and one of our nuclear subs. Nixon's expertise and knowledge in the programming response data on board that sub is imperative to averting a catastrophic disaster."

Cronin rose to the occasion. "I understand," he said, his features tightening. "I'll have you out of here so quickly you'll think you're in the hundred-meter finals at the Olympics."

Lemons nodded to his escorts as Cronin flew into action.

"Patch me through to Flight 515," he said, addressing his two-way radio. The static-laden answer appeared to satisfy him. "Good. Flight 515, I want passenger Nixon, row 22, seat B, transported to the door. When the hatch opens, I want him the first one off. First! You got it?"

"Yes, sir," came the answer.

Cronin tapped in a second frequency. "Ground Ops," he said.

"Go ahead," came the response.

"Ground Ops, this is Charles Cronin. I want a vehicle at the lower level of Concourse A, immediately. See that it's clear to go as soon as I arrive. And shut down escalator 11C in both directions at baggage claim. You got that?"

"Got it, will do, sir."

Cronin had begun to breathe heavily from the excitement.

Lemons gave a wary look to Jenkins and Thomas.

"Patch me back to 515," Cronin directed the radio operator.

"Yes, sir."

"Flight 515, Cronin again."

"Yes, sir, go ahead please."

"Has passenger Nixon checked any baggage?"

After a few seconds, the response came. "That's affirmative, sir. Two items. You want the ID numbers?"

"Yes."

"OK, we have DL 4763 and DL 4764—both under forty pounds. No other description."

"That's fine. Thank you."

Cronin was fired up. He tapped in one more frequency. "Ground crew, Charles Cronin speaking."

After a pause, someone came on the line. "That you again, Buck? Get off the line and quit playing around."

"This is Charles Cronin from Delta!" Cronin announced sharply. "Who am I speaking to?"

There was silence for a moment or two. Then a response came, "Yes, sir, this is Barrone. What can I do for you, sir?"

"I need two pieces of luggage out of Flight 515. Need ID# DL 4763 and DL4764," Cronin instructed. "I want them at the carousel as soon as that plane touches down. Do you hear me? I don't want them mixed in, I don't want them floating up the conveyor, I want them hand carried as fast as your legs can carry you, to Carousel Six, Barrone. Got it?"

"Yes, sir," Barrone responded. "I'm on it. Right away."

Just then, had Lemons been alert, he would have heard a slight rustling of paper fifteen yards away. Fitz retrieved her cellular phone, pressed the redial button, and held it to her ear. "Hold please," was all she said.

Moments later, when the first passenger emerged from the Gate Eleven runway, she sat up straight. "Now!" she said into the phone.

With the attention of Lemons, Thomas and Jenkins focused on the arrival of Mr. Nixon, Fitz was able to rapidly retreat and disappear down the concourse completely undetected. With her command, the timing device had just been set.

Charles Cronin approached Mike Nixon and headed him toward the waiting three. "Mr. Nixon," he said, "This is Mr. Lemons, Mr. Jenkins, and Mr. Thomas."

Mr. Nixon appeared startled.

"There's no time for lengthy introductions," began Lemons. "Mr. Nixon, we are instructed to get you to Atlanta headquarters for an important top secret defense teleconference." He directed his attention to Cronin. "Mr.

Cronin, you and Mr. Thomas take the lead. I'll escort Mr. Nixon, and Jenkins, you bring up the rear. Let's go!"

The group was off at a rapid pace on foot. Jenkins spoke into his cell phone. "Driver, we're about five minutes away."

"There appears to be some back-up with security. They are checking some baggage. Additionally, I see two suspicious characters outside the baggage claim. I'll keep you posted."

Jenkins relayed the information he received to the others.

"I'll handle it," Cronin said. Addressing his radio again, he puffed out, "Cronin to security. Come in."

"Yes, sir."

"I need additional security stat for baggage check at the doors near Carousel Six. I also need someone at that entranceway. Immediately!"

By that time, the group was rapidly approaching the stilled escalators. At the bottom, they jumped into the waiting vehicle and with lights flashing, traveled as rapidly as circumstances allowed to Carousel Six, just missing the first flashing of the sign, *Welcome to Atlanta! Home of the 1995 Peach Bowl & 1996 Olympic Games!*

At Carousel Six, two pieces of luggage traveled in lonely circles. Thomas and Jenkins snatched them up. Lemons thanked Cronin for his help, and four men exited, jumping into the waiting limousine.

Cronin bent over, hands on his knees, gasping for air. "You're welcome," he wheezed toward the disappearing limo, "anytime."

Tim and the Train stood under cover of some large ornamental boxwoods.

"Shit," said Tim, snapping off the timing device.

The two dispirited professionals walked toward the public parking facility. They knew that later that night, they would suffer great embarrassment and pay dearly for their missed calculations.

Chapter Two
Yellow Jacket Bar

Not far away, Fitz, satisfied, prepared to rendezvous later with the organization.

Meanwhile, the limousine headed north on I-85, passing the freshly created Olympic Stadium, ready for the games. Just after, it exited onto Peachtree Street, covered the couple of blocks and turned onto North Avenue. There, it approached the famous 1928-established world's largest fast food refectory, The Varsity, which seats 800 and provides parking for 600.

The Varsity has a language all its own. "What'll ya have?" the counter servers demand.

"I'll have a heavyweight, sideways. Bag of rags, and squeeze one!" comes the answer. The customer has just requested a hot dog with extra chili, onions on the side, a bag of chips, and a Varsity orange drink.

A traditional drive-in graces the parking area, in which waiters take orders and deliver the famed cuisine to patrons sitting in their cars.

The vehicle crossed the Downtown Connector. Georgia Institute of Technology, an internationally known university, boasting 150 countries worth of alumni and current students, is situated on the avenue next, just before Bobby Dodd Stadium to the right. On the left, sat Roosevelt Towers, a large senior citizen home, affectionately referred to by the locals as a retirement community. On the same side of street, lies the eight-story Berger dormitory and then the Yellow Jackets Bar and Restaurant. Not far away, but at the pinnacle of the ensuing rise on North Avenue, the famed and glorious Coca Cola Bottling Company is situated.

The limo pulled up alongside Roosevelt Towers. The sophisticated Mr. Thomas rose from his seat in the back and appeared to undergo an unprecedented metamorphosis. Tossing his sunglasses, tie, and jacket in a pile, he jumped from the car and, leaning against the front fender, began to chant toward a balcony on the top floor.

"Yo! Yo, fart! Yo!"

Unaccustomed eyebrows in the neighborhood rose, hearts bearing ill-will to the disrespectful upstart in the fancy car.

Before long, the other four tossed off their accessories and joined him, Lemons in a deep baritone.

"Yo, fart!"

In due time, an elderly face appeared, leaning over the balcony. It was grinning. "How'd we make out?" he rasped.

Five thumbs were raised high in the air.

"Tops, McBride!" yelled Harry Thomas. "We are the best!"

"All right men! I'll meet ya down the street in half an hour!" McBride called out.

Harry Thomas, aka "Mr. Thomas," was the president and leader of the organization. As a Georgia Tech MBA student, he applied his knowledge to the group's shenanigans, and vice versa.

Harry's cohort, Joe Jenkins, "Mr. Jenkins," an electrical engineering student at Georgia Tech took great pleasure in any good gag. He was the only Texan in the group, and other than on rare occasions, such as that very day, he was not without his cowboy hat. Joe had assisted McBride in the amazing feat of connecting the old coach to the live, play by play of the football team. This had been accomplished in the creation of a mobile and highly functional transmitter, both receiving and relaying signals from an earpiece/mouthpiece McBride wore, usually attached to his baseball cap. His participation was further enhanced by the use of a high-powered telescope, mounted appropriately on the older man's balcony. He was "in the game."

Joe and Harry's impressive leader in the airport was exactly who he said he was, Marvin Lemons. A sixty-seven-year-old retired police officer, Marvin had given a lifetime of good years to the force, many in the upper echelons of the Atlanta Metro Police Department. He had since enjoyed the frivolity of the mischievously enticing organization created by Harry, *the Fraternity Among Retirees and Tech Students*, or, more familiarly referred to by its acronym, FARTs.

Their "computer expert" was, in fact, just that. Mike Nixon was a computer science major at Tech, widely considered, by his professors and classmates alike, a genius. His expertise was unparalleled in hacking, devising formulae, and program writing.

The limo driver, the athletically built Gary Sowell, was a structural engineering student at Georgia Tech. A native of the Atlanta suburbs and part-time limo driver, he had developed quite a working knowledge of the city streets ins and outs.

The object of the group's visit, Jack McBride was a 73-year-old retiree resident of Roosevelt Towers. A native, too, of Atlanta, he had left the city in 1944 with the U.S. Army for Europe to go fight the Germans. But earlier in the 1940s, Jack had attended Georgia Tech and played varsity basketball for two years.

There were nine male members in all. Three others waited at headquarters, formally known as the Yellow Jacket. Dave Schwelfer, more commonly known as "Mr. Beer," also lived at Roosevelt Towers. At the age of 71, he was still quite capable of drinking anyone under the table, young or old.

And as far as anyone can remember, the man has never been drunk.

His 72-year-old buddy, Bob Arnold, was another regular at the Yellow Jacket and also resided in nearby Roosevelt Towers. Bob's famed nickname, "Boner," was a familiar chant whenever he entered the bar. He took pride in the moniker.

Finally, 48-year-old Theodore Anderson, nicknamed Ted, but known to the fellows as "Buzz," came from a wealthy family in the Buckhead section of Atlanta. Buzz had excelled in gymnastics and by the time he'd graduated in 1969, he had become captain of the gymnastics team. He became even more well-known, however, for his patented back flip as the University's mascot. In full bumblebee costume, he would hang out on the sidelines and during basketball games. If Tech was moving in the path of victory, the spectators would get excited, and start buzzing until Buzz obliged with his back flip from either the cross bar or basketball hoop. He never once failed to make a perfect landing.

Buzz, like Jack, was a veteran. Unlike Jack, however, he never discussed his experiences of war. To him, it seemed, those years had never happened. When he returned to the United States, Buzz took a job with the Coca Cola Company and rose quickly to a position in middle management. But Buzz had no interest in furthering his career, which meant leaving the Atlanta area.

His wardrobe and countenance read like a GQ cover, while some of his gestures tended to suggest he was a little light in the loafers. Buzz never married, and lived alone on Peachtree Street across from the Fox Theatre. His frequency at the Yellow Jacket, mixed with his specially concocted formula, had earned him a drink named after him in the history of the Yellow Jacket Bar & Restaurant—Buzz's In and Out Birdbath Martini. Specifically, it was comprised of one chilled martini glass, a swirled and discarded swallow's worth of vermouth, a fill-up with Stolichnaya Vodka, three olives at the bottom, and a swipe of freshly oiled lemon peel, which was then discarded. It was a daily regimen, and always his last drink of the night. Buzz's business day ran from 7:00 am to 3:30 pm.

That afternoon, at 3:45 pm, he was already deep in conversation with Dave "Mr. Beer" Schwelfer.

Margaret "Fitz" Fitzpatrick Beckley wore a well-earned smile on her face as she ordered her first drink.

"So it went off like clockwork, huh?" asked Marta Rives, Georgia Tech's former hope of women's basketball. She'd injured her knee early in her college career, but Tech honored her scholarship even with her sidelined. That afternoon, she shared a table near the male *F.A.R.T.S.* with the rest of the honorary sorority of *F.A.R..T.S,* affectionately referred to by the much preferred nickname, '*ettes*,' for *F.A.R.T.S-ettes.*

Fitz, the celebrated female *F.A.R..T.S.* winked at her 70-year-old compadre from the hospital floors, Charlotte Gaffney. "Any of you guys could have done it," she said. "You wouldn't believe it! But don't let on like you know. The guys want Tim to announce it good and proper."

Maggie Hacket giggled. She thought of Harry Thomas, her close friend and one-time lover. "I wish I could have seen it!" she said.

"It was something," Fitz went on. "The guy in charge of ops at Delta had a bit of a tummy. He started puffing and panting before they'd even started racing him around the airport!"

The bar maintained a pretty good crowd under normal circumstances, but that evening, it would fill quickly and stay that way. The Peach Bowl had brought not only staff and athletes' families, but spectators, too, had begun to arrive.

"Yeah, this is the place," Dave Schwelfer called to any patrons with looks of curiosity on their faces.

"Hey, you need a job?" the bartender called. "I'm sure I could get you on the PR payroll!"

Dave smiled. "I put in my fifty years," he said smiling warmly. "I like my life just fine where I am. But I sure appreciate the offer."

The bartender chuckled.

"People always trying to get you into their bars, huh?" Buzz asked, teasing his old friend.

"Yeah, somebody's always trying to get me drunk!" Dave joked.

His eyes came to rest on the wall of athletes gone by, arranged haphazardly across the bar wall. Georgia Tech had its share of boasting material; not only esteemed athletes and teams, but astronauts, business leaders, and savvy politicians. The photo Dave studied that afternoon was the one of his buddy Buzz in his Georgia Tech bumblebee mascot getup. The younger man had been photographed some thirty years before as he performed his signature back flip.

"You looking at those guys?" Buzz teased, pointing at the two separate frames. The only two that did not belong to the Georgia Tech alumni were of Tim Ecclestone, Jersey #14, and Eric "The Train" Vail, both of whom played for NHL's Atlanta Flames. Tim and his wife, Sue, had moved down from Canada to purchase the Yellow Jacket Bar ten years before.

"Yeah, two funny-sounding Canadian men really get me hot, ay?" Dave answered.

"Hey, listen," Buzz continued, "to each his own. Ay."

"Shit, ay?" said Dave.

Buzz laughed out loud and slapped his buddy on the back. "Another beer for my buddy!" he called.

"Hey, look, Gary and Mike are here," Dave said. "And they got Jack and Harry with'em. Yo F.A.R.T.S.! Over here!"

Mike's head shot up. "There they are!" he said, nudging Gary. "You save us a spot, old man?"

"You'll be old one day, too," said a middle-aged woman overhearing him.

Mike smiled sheepishly. "Sorry, ma'am."

She nodded and returned to her conversation.

"Yeah, Mike," Harry joined in, stifling a laugh, "watch your mouth!"

"Come on over here, guys," Buzz said as they got closer. "We saved you a spot."

"Boy have we got a story for you!" Mike began.

"Uh uh uh! Hold it!" Gary said. "Not everybody's here, yet. Wait 'til we're all here."

"Good or bad?" Dave asked.

"I'm sticking to the code," Gary answered. "All for one and one for all."

"You can't change 'em," Mike said raising his hands to either side of his head. "Might as well forget it. Hey, there's Fitz and them! You talk to them yet, guys?"

"Not yet. Let's buy 'em a round. Hey Eric!" Dave pretended to be an irate customer. "Aren't you the manager here? I can't get a single drink! What does it take?"

Eric approached from a small doorway behind the bar. "Hey, quiet down. We got sophisticated customers in here."

"What's that mean? The kind that can count higher than a hundred?" Gary jibed.

"Well, I don't want to mislead you guys," Eric said, "but I'm pretty sure they can make it past twelve."

"Have a good day, Eric?" Mike asked.

"Hey, Nixon, can it!" Gary said. "Nothing 'til we're all here."

Eric shook his head and motioned to the bartender. "Watch these guys," he said. "If they get out of control, flag 'em all."

Mike, Gary, Harry, and Jack chuckled quietly.

"How 'bout a round for our lady friends at the table over there," Buzz said. "You can put it on his tab." He pointed to Dave.

"And you can put my tab," Dave countered, "on his tab."

"Same with mine," came a voice to their right.

"Boner!" Gary shouted.

At that, the regulars at the Yellow Jacket rallied. "Boner! Boner! Boner!"

Bob "Boner" nodded appreciatively to the group, took a seat, and said officiously, "Thank you. As you were."

Tex, who had come in with Boner took a seat. "How come nobody says, 'Tex! Tex! Tex!' when I come into the place?" he asked.

"It don't flow," explained Gary. "You gotta have two syllables. Now, if you went by Texas, well, it just might happen. I'm not saying it will, but it might. Hey listen…"

But Tex had taken the few minutes to unzip the soft case protecting his vintage trombone. Since grade school, he'd been one with the instrument. That night, he decided it would be a good night to provide the bar with the Georgia Tech fight song.

"OK, guy," Harry said, laughing. "Look at this guy, Buzz. You ever see anything like it?"

Tex blasted out the melody, prancing around the bar with his trombone held high as the crowd fell in with the words:

I'm a ramblin' wreck from Georgia Tech
And a hell of an engineer,
A helluva, helluva, helluva helluva,
Hell of an engineer.
Like all the jolly good fellows,
I drink my whiskey clear.
I'm a ramblin' wreck from Georgia Tech
And a hell of an engineer.
Oh, if I had a daughter, Sir,

I'd dress her in white and gold,
And put her on campus,
To cheer the Brave and Bold.
But if I had a son, Sir,
I'll tell you what he'd do.
He would yell "To Hell with Georgia,"
Just like his daddy used to do.
Oh, I wish I had a barrel,
Of rum and sugar three thousand pounds,
A college bell to put it in,
And a clapper to stir it around,
I'd drink to all good fellows
Who come from far and near.
I'm a ramblin' gamblin' hell of an engineer.

Long Standing Traditional

Newcomers were astounded by the performance, feeling as if they'd possibly stumbled into a rehearsal of some kind. Seeing no cameras, or lights, however, the joined in the best they could and clapped when the performance was over.

"I think you make up for not being announced when you come in just fine, Tex," Buzz said, laughing.

Suddenly Eric was motioning for quiet. "Please, please, everyone," he said waving his arms. "Can I have your attention please?"

Quickly the room quieted down and Eric cleared his throat. The *F.A.R.T.S.* smiled at one another, anticipating the announcement.

But once it was perfectly quiet, all Eric said was, "OK Tex! One more time!"

The bar burst into raucous laughter, the trombone blasting above it all, as the song was sung again, the second time absent quite a few of the actual lyrics, which were replaced with improvised thoughts by the singers—not all of which were charitable.

Buzz rose to his position on the bar, buzzing as he had done in Georgia Tech mascot days. Toward the end of the song, Eric reached for the house P.A.

"OK, everybody, I must insist that you all close your eyes. Our in-house Yellow Jacket mascot will perform his tamest back flip. But he must have complete concentration. That means you must close your eyes, and if I could have the assistance of the patrons at the bar? We need a drum roll, please."

The atmosphere was tense; a mixture of the unknowing and those near exploding with laughter.

Once all—or mostly all—eyes were closed, Buzz carefully climbed down from the bar, and stood in perfect landing position.

"He did it!" cried Dave. "He did it!"

Everyone opened their eyes and started to buzz, a corollary of Georgia Tech folks to victory of any kind. Buzz smiled widely, and jogged a victory lap around the bar, high-fiving and taking smacks on the back.

Boner sidled up to Jack. "He didn't actually do it, did he?"

Jack burst out laughing. "You know, Boner, you could be a hundred years old and still as gullible as the day you were born!"

"Well, I was just asking…" his old friend said mildly with a smile.

By 8:00 pm, the *F.A.R.T.S.* were out of patience. It was time for the real announcement.

"As you all know," Eric began, "some of us are simply superior to others."

A few giggles rippled through the nearby cluster of tables where the members of the organization had congregated.

"Oh, get on with it!" Tim called from the doorway.

Tim rose. "I would like to take the opportunity to review with you the facts."

All members applauded in approval, and were joined by some uninformed, yet enthusiastic others.

"As you know, with over nine hundred dollars in the pot, it came time to do something about it. As Canadians—and owner and manager of this establishment, we felt it necessary to question the aptitude, nay, the depth of capacity and potency of the *F.A.R.T.S.*"

The bar erupted with laughter.

Tim raised one hand in the air. "Please," he said with a serious expression on his face. "Allow me to proceed uninterrupted."

The laughter wound down to a few titters and a cough.

"It came down to a bet," Tim continued. "Could the *F.A.R.T.S.* manage to transport one of their very own members through Hartsfield International Airport, bearing at least two pieces of checked luggage, traveling coach, and utilizing concourse A, B, C, or D in less than fifteen minutes?"

He paused for drama. "And what do you think? Could it be done?"

Silence then filled the bar, everyone's attention riveted on the Canadian bacon standing at table six. He sighed. "Alas…yes!"

Applause and cheers burst throughout the bar. Over the commotion, Tim shouted, "You bet they could! No pun intended. They nailed that sucker! In and out in six minutes, thirty-two seconds!"

"Hey, and I drove!" Gary called out. "I was the driver!"

"That was afterwards," Buzz called through the din.

"Yeah, but I drove—I made it look realistic!" Gary insisted.

"Yeah, OK, Gary," Dave said.

"Really!" Gary insisted. "Listen, guys."

"I'll listen if you buy me a beer," Dave said.

"How 'bout this?" Gary said, trying a different tack. "My dad's best friend, Mike Curtis, has a super box on the 50-Yard Line at the Dome. They'll be out of town with my parents during the Peach Bowl. Guess who gets to use it?"

That got Dave's attention. "No shit?"

"Yeah. It holds twenty-four—open bar, bartender included."

"I'm in!" Dave answered.

"We'll all go," Buzz added, "if you got the space."

"Yeah, all of us!" Gary said, finally happy to get everyone's attention.

Buzz wandered over the table of *ettes*. He was a regular visitor to the women's quarters, often offering reviews of books they might be interested in or swapping recipes—even offering opinions on good choices for needlepoint. Quite often, he picked up the ladies' tab, as well.

"Look at you," said Fitz.

"Me? What's the matter?" Buzz asked, sitting back. "What did I do?"

"There you are, at work before 7:00 am. You go till 3:30 pm, have six or eight beers, jump around like a dancing bee, have two vodka martinis equaling six of normal size…"

Buzz looked even more perplexed as her voice trailed off. "What? *What?*"

"You don't have a wrinkle! Not a single one! Your hair is perfectly in place, clothes are neat and fresh, you even smell good! It's as if you just stepped out of the shower."

Buzz raised his hands, palms up, without saying a word.

"Are all gays that way?" Fitz went on. "Or forget it. You're not gay, you're… you're crispy," she finished.

Buzz stood up in mock dismay, covering his cheeks with his hands. "Well!" he shrieked, "I have been called a lot of things in my life! But I will not allow anyone to call me 'crispy'!"

Nearby, Swank Weeks sat with his wife, Jane. Swank had been a regular at the Yellow Jacket during his days at Tech in the early '70s. Jane had been a cheerleader for the blue and gold. Long fascinated by the university and its strong subculture, Jane and Swank never missed a game, and often graced the sidelines of the amusing but usually baffling *F.A.R.T.S.* exchanges. Earlier, comfortable from the evening's refreshments, Jane had accepted Buzz's offer to join him on the bar; as he buzzed, she cheered.

As Buzz headed back to the bar, Swank snagged him with a question that had long plagued his curious mind. "Why do you guys call each other 'farts'?"

"Oh, well, that's because we are all members of the same farternity."

"What? What's that?"

Buzz chuckled. "You know, a group. It stands for Farternity Among Retirees and Tech Students. We've been around a few years now. As you've probably noticed, there's a pretty big age range in the membership!"

"Yeah—well, to be honest, we can't really tell who's who. I mean it seems like the bartenders, or the manager, and who else?"

"Actually, the group consists of nine—older retirees, Tech students, and then there's me. We love to razz Eric and Tim, but officially, they're not part of the Farternity. We also have a kind of honorary group called the *F.A.R.T.-ettes*, but they prefer to hang back. We refer to them as the 'ettes,' out of courtesy."

"I can see why. But how in the world did such an unlikely group get together?" Swank asked.

"It's a cute story," Buzz said, sitting back in the chair. "You'll like this."

Chapter Three
September, 1993

Buzz adjusted into a more comfortable position and his eyes grew distant with the reverie. "It was about three years ago," he began. "This same bar. Couple of us were sitting at the bar. I guess there must have been about thirty or forty people in all. It was kind of in-between lunch and happy hour. A guy comes up and sits next to a middle-aged black guy in a suit. He says, 'Hey, how ya doin'? I'm Mike Nixon.'

"The black guy shakes his hand, checking him out, and says, 'Marvin Lemons. Good to know you.'

"Well, Mike went on, you know, talking about the place and what he thought of the nice warm weather in Atlanta. And he asks Mr. Lemons, 'So, are you connected with the university? Georgia Tech?'

Marvin leans back and he says, 'Nah, I just do a little security now and then. The games, you know. I like the old school well enough, but I come here mainly because I live just down the street, there.'

"'Is that right. Well, I've just been here as much as four hours myself,' Mike answered. 'Got myself a transfer from MIT, up north. Yeah, this is nice down here.'

"'Oh, yeah,' Marvin answered him. 'I always like the south, myself.'

"Just then, they started to notice a group of about eight kids across the bar from then getting pretty rowdy. They were all preppie types, in their sport jackets and open collared shirts—one even had a tie up over his shoulder."

Buzz paused to laugh at the memory. Swank joined in.

"Now why did they do that?" Swank asked. "I always wondered about that."

"Probably wanted to show that they were always on the move," Buzz said, laughing, "you know, the tie is flying back like that?"

"That's the first logical explanation I've ever heard to that," Swank said.

"Well, anyway," Buzz went on, "these smart ass kids were starting to act obnoxious. For whatever reason, they start knocking the old fellows down the end of the bar.

"'Hey, old geezer,' one of 'em says, 'you got a permission slip to be out this late?'

"You know, real obnoxious stuff. And they went on and on. This kid, Mike is sitting here and he's getting real burnt about it.

"'Hey, knock it off!' he goes, 'What's the matter? You guys just having your first beers over there? Is the excitement all too much for you?'

"'What's it to you?' the real outspoken one says. 'Mind your own business!'

"Then there's a kid on the other side of Mike, guy by the name of Harry Thomas—I'm sure you've seen him around. Anyway, he goes, 'Oh, get over yourself, Buff.'

"Well, Buff wasn't gonna have any underclassman pushing him around. He stands up and says 'Any time you and your buddies are big enough, come on over!'"

"'Holy shit,' Mike says, 'Less than twenty-four hours in the state of Georgia and here I am in my first fight!' And he and Harry start to get up.

"But just as they do, they feel the hand of this Marvin Lemons on their shoulders, something like a vice grip—but a kindly vice grip. 'Sit down,' he says, 'Don't you see what's going on?'

"'Yeah, I see what's going on,' Harry says, 'a couple of smartass cowards are giving their bullshit routine to a couple of fellows who can't defend themselves.'

"'Don't be so sure,' Marvin says. 'Them old boys are doing just fine. Have a seat and watch what's going on. Look over there.'

"Marvin nods in the direction of the men's room. 'See that?'

"Mike and Harry looked in the direction he indicated and saw a short fellow, who was Bob Arnold, discreetly lift up two mugs of beer and disappear into the men's room.

"'What's he doing?' Mike asks Marvin.

"'Every time those upstarts make one of their remarks, he visits the men's room and dunks his gonads in their beer—special prep, you might say.'

"'Gonads?' Mike says, 'What's gonads?'

"Old Marvin reared back, trying to keep his laughter in check—'It's your *dipstick!*' he says in a loud whisper.

"That got Mike and Harry started, and they did the best they could to keep it under control, but it sure gave them new respect for the old fellows down the bar.

'Watch this guy,' Mavin went on, pointing to Dave Schwelfer, 'you won't believe this!'

"Dave stood up, leaned back, and somehow—and trust me, Swank, he really did this," Buzz said. "I should know—I was standing right next to him at the time. He throws his voice and bellows out, 'Bartender! Give everybody in the place a drink on me!'

"So the Bartender goes right to it—he serves us all another of what we're having (except me, because I hadn't started yet), and then he goes and takes the anti from the stash in front of old Buff!" Buzz laughed at the recollection.

"What did they do?" Swank asked.

"You mean the preppies?" Buzz asked. "They couldn't do anything. The Bartender made the call and that was that. Not unless they wanted to get cut off. To tell you the truth, I think they were half-gone anyway.

"Meanwhile, there were a couple girls hanging around with these preppies," Buzz continued, "and it was right around then that they decided to hit the ladies room. Bob Arnold, that little leprechaun, decided he wasn't quite finished wrecking havoc with the obnoxious group. He coordinated with Jack, and just at the right time, one of them killed the lights in the ladies room, while the other punched in a loud tune on the jukebox. The girls in the ladies room must have been screaming like mad, but nobody heard it!

"By that time, you can bet Harry Thomas and Mike Nixon were starting to get quite an appreciation for the old guys. But they weren't done yet!

"'Watch this!' says Lemons. 'Here comes the big sting.'

"You can bet Mike and Harry were enjoying the show. The next thing they know, Jack McBride starts air golfing—showing off his swing to Bob. But it's not a good swing, you know what I mean? It's kind of amateur looking. And boy does that start the preppies up again. Their girls had just about all gotten back from the ladies room, telling those guys all about what happened with the lights, and these guys still had no clue they were being played like fiddles.

"'Yeah, some swing there, oldtimer,' one of Buff's buddies starts in. 'Are you a contender for the mini-golf championship?'

"'Got yourself a mighty swing,' Buff says. 'Kinda reminds me of Mighty Mouse.'

"All the preppies start laughing and throwing out insults. But McBride keeps on, kinda acting like he doesn't really know they're making fun of him.

"Then one of the gang says, 'Hey, ever play for money, old man?'

"And Jack's totally cool about it. 'All the time,' he says.

"'Oh yeah? How much? Fifty cents? A buck?'

"'Sometimes two bucks,' Jack answers seriously.

"The whole crowd of preppies laughs louder still. 'You save up your pennies, old man,' the kid cries, 'and when we can tee it up for a hundred dollars a hole, you give me a call.'

"'Woah!' McBride answered. 'That's a lot of money.'

"'It's chicken feed,' said the kid.

"'Well, tell me, young fellow,' Jack went on, 'how do we adjust the handicaps?'

"'Hey hey hey, no handicaps!' the kid yelled back across the bar. 'You can't play, don't try to make it with the big boys. Just tee it high, and let it fly!'

"So I'm listening in, and I can't resist. I called out, 'Hey—is that bet open to anyone?' And he tries to burn me, he goes, 'I was talking about playing against the old man over there. Not you, cupcake!'

"But I kept at him. 'No,' I explained, 'I'm not talking about playing against you, I just want to get in on the bet.' Well that got him interested. Everybody loves easy money.

"He says, 'I don't give a shit where the money comes from—long as it's cash.'

"So I asked Jack McBride if he minded if I put two hundred dollars on him. He gave me the green light just before Dave Schwelfer calls out, 'Put me down for a hundred!' And Bob Arnold jumps in, too. 'I'm in for a hundred.' Then Marvin Lemons across the bar calls out, 'Count me in for a hundred.' 'Well, I guess I better put a hundred in myself,' Jack said.

"Meanwhile Tex Jenkins and Gary Sowell had sat down at the bar next to the other students. Marvin Lemons turns to the group of four students. 'There was an article in the paper about Jack McBride. It was hanging right there at the Roosevelt Towers. It says McBride shoots his age.'

"So Tex Jenkins calls across to McBride, 'Sir, how old are you?'

"'I'm seventy-one," Jack said proudly. That got the kids at the bar next to Lemons started. 'Can I put in fifty dollars?' Mike Nixon asks, and same with Gary Sowell and

Harry Thomas. And Tex says, 'If I can find a place to cash my check, you count me in for fifty bucks, too.'

"Meanwhile Eric, the bar manager was listening to all this. He's nodding. 'I'll cash that check for ya, buddy. And put me in for a hundred fifty.'

"It was great," Buzz went on, "people were calling out from everywhere. Then this older lady at a booth chimes in. 'I have fifty dollars for the pot!' We all turn around and she's shaking the bills at us at the bar. And Mike Nixon, paying close attention to the sum announced right then, 'OK—that's a thousand bucks, smart ass. Are you ready?'

"Well, the whole tone of these kids changed then. They've got nice allowances, but a thousand bucks—losing that would hurt, at least for a while. But they were pretty confident anyway.

"'When do you want to play?' the kid asks. 'In a week or two?'

"McBride answers, 'I prefer right now. We can tee it high and let it fly at Bobby Jones Golf Course. It's only five minutes away and we can get nine holes in, no problem.'

"Well, I guess those boys felt the tables were turning, but they had more pride than they knew what to do with. And as soon as Mike and the guys started sticking it to them to put up or shut up, they had a few more things to say.

"Buff started out with, 'My man is the club champ at Atlanta Country Club. He's one of the best golfers in the state. We don't want to take your money.'

"And Joe Jenkins goes, 'Oh you all are nothin' but a pack of pussies—scuse my language,' he said, turning to Fitz.

"'No problem,' she says resolutely. 'I think that describes the bunch of 'em to a T.'

"It was all starting to come down on those preppies, then," Buzz went on. "Everyone had something to say, and they started to feel very defensive. 'We got our money up,' Bob Arnold told them, 'It's time you boys put your money where your mouth is.'

"That was enough for Buff, who simply could not deal with a bunch of old guys making them look like idiots. 'OK,' he says, 'you're on! The match will start at 6:30. We play where it lies, no mulligans, no handicaps, just straight match play. One hundred buck per hole. If the hole is a tie, the money carries over to the next. And one hundred dollars for the match.' He let out a breath of air like he'd just finished the hundred yard dash.

"Marvin Lemons looks at the guys next to him and says coolly, 'Gentlemen, that's the easiest money you ever made.'

"'How can you be so sure?' Gary asks him.

"'Well let me tell you. Jack McBride hits that course everyday. He knows every blade of grass at that Bobby Jones course. That loudmouth mama's boy over there might have a chance if the wager involved his Atlanta Country Club course—but not at Bobby Jones. And here's something else. Most guys hang at the bar all day and their swing gets lousy. But the more McBride drinks, the better he gets!'

"And Gary and Mike smile at each other. Then everybody meets out at the course. McBride's getting his things together and the head pro at the shop there asks him,

"Who ya playin' today, Jack?'

"McBride nods in the direction of the preppie warming up. 'That dude over there,' he says.

"'Woah! That's Billy Hodges,' the guy tells him. 'He finished third in the State Amateur Championship. The kid's one of the best golfers in the south.'

"Buff was listening and loving it. 'I told you he was good,' he gloated, 'do you wanna cancel the bet? There's still time.'

"McBride played along like the dotty old fellow, you know? The kind that doesn't really know quite what's going on, but hangs in there? Anyway, he says something like, 'Oh no! I'm too old to give up. You know, it would bother me the rest of my life if I didn't try—I'd never know whether I could beat the young fellow or not.'

"Buff just shook his head. I could tell he was a little concerned, but he was trying to act like he had developed some concern for Jack. Anyway, after that, he asked the head pro to officiate the match for them. 'We'll each throw in twenty bucks,' he says.

"'Fine with me,' McBride says.

"'Love to!' the head pro answers. He closed up shop and off we went.

"I drove along in Dave Schwelfer's golf cart, which he had thoughtfully filled with a cooler of beer, and a quart container of martinis for me. I hadn't had time to change, so I stood up in back, in my coat and tie, in a great observation spot.

"The first four holes were interesting. Overall, I guess the kid Hodges out drove Jack by sixty yards. Yet, Jack was two under par and leading the clown four to zero. Hodges warmed up a little and managed to tie the next three holes with Jack, both hitting par. Then, they get to the eighth tee. McBride must have been feeling a little sorry for the kid, or maybe he was just playing, I don't know. But he leans over and says to him, 'Listen, if you use your driver, you're gonna put it in that lake. It's three hundred twenty yards down the fairway, but you're gonna do it just the same. Just a word of advice.'

"'If I need your help, I'll ask for it, old man!' Hodges snapped. And he takes out his driver, just to be defiant. And guess what happens? The ball soars straight down the middle, and after two bounces, it rolls right into the water.

"By the start of the ninth hole, McBride's team had already won nine hundred bucks. Jack looks over at Bob Arnold and asks, 'You think I ought to go a little easy on him on the last hole?'

"Arnold minced no words. 'Fuck 'em,' he said.

"And that was that," Buzz chuckled. "It didn't take long to end the drama. The boys did pay up, to their credit, and, not surprisingly, headed for the hills. I don't think they hit the Yellow Jacket again, at least not as group.

"But anyway, it was after that incident that the *F.A.R.T.*s began. We all headed back to the bar to divvy up the kitty. There were four students from Georgia Tech, four retirees, and me. And also Fitz over there, she'd come along, too. We kind of hit it off. Marvin Lemons had sort of known the older fellows from their shenanigans at Roosevelt Towers where they live. On that night, they became much closer friends, too.

"It really turned out great in a lot of ways. Mike's first day turned not only into a cash winning one, but also new friends on campus. He'd seen his room, and hadn't thought much of it.

"'I'm gonna have to back into it,' he laughed to Harry Thomas. 'I'm not sure I'll be able to go in there forwards carrying anything. When I want to get into bed, I'm going to have to learn to levitate to get over the boxes.

"Harry was laughing. 'Listen,' he said seriously, 'how would you like a job as floor monitor in the dorm one over from yours? I'm supposed to run things at Burge Dormitory there, and Tex—you know, Joe, and Gary here are each monitors of one floor. Why not you? It'll get you a private room and fifty bucks a month. All you gotta do for it is basically hang around at certain times and—

"'I'll take it, I'll take it!' Mike cuts in.

"It was the beginning of a really great thing, and as we all went on, Fitz's friend joins her, and somehow, they ended up talking with two college-aged girls, too. It was great. They say kids can sometimes talk to their grandparents about certain things more easily than they can their parents. I think that must have been true for us, because things really came together, starting that night.

"And we really were more than just drinking buddies. In fact, the very next day, Harry, Gary, and Tex helped Mike move into his new room. They came over here afterwards and they started talking.

"'So you were a computer major at MIT, huh?' Gary asked him. 'How good are you?'

"'Let's see, I broke George Tech's code earlier today…'

"'What do you mean, broke the code?' Harry asked. 'Broke the code in terms of what?'

"'I mean I can hack in. Anything they've got in there, I can access. For example, say I want to see the schedule they've got me set up for this fall. OK, I get in via the codes I broke earlier, go the department and type in my name. And it comes on the screen.'

"'No shit!' said Gary. 'So you could change your grade and everything!'

"'No, no, no—I *could*, but I won't. Don't ask me to do anything like that. That ain't right. But I could add a few things to a resume, or move a class around, that kind of thing.'

"So the next day, they go over to Mike's new place. I wasn't there, but they decided to call up Harry's student record. Harry wanted to be the President of the group we'd put together here, and he wanted the office on his record. His problem was that if the club he was president of was not an officially recognized Georgia Tech activity, then it couldn't appear on his record. So they're messing around with names and of course that's when they came up with "Farternity Among Retirees and Tech Students—what's the acronym? You got it! *F.A.R.T.S.* Before you know it, Mike's that the long name for that organization registered as an official Georgia Tech activity—and guess who's president?"
Swank laughed. "That's too much!"

"Yeah, and it's still registered. Harry's still the President. They spent a little more time messing with Buff's schedule. I think they were kind enough to give him a five-hour lab on Saturday at 7:00 am, you know that kind of thing. But another thing that happened then and there was the establishment of what you might call our club's headquarters.

"Harry decided that he'd take these guys to the roof of Burger dormitory and tell them his dream for it. 'I'd like to set up a private roof garden up here,' he told them.

"'Look at that view!' Gary said. 'You can see downtown—and there's the stadium right across North Avenue. You could have members only football parties here during the season.'

"'Yeah,' Harry answered. 'You know, I was reading a book over the summer about World War II. One of the spy headquarters for the Germans was called *The Up There*. I think we should call this *The Up There*.'

"And they all agree, but Tex can't resist. 'So I'll ask you, Harry, where are you headed? And you say, The Up There. And I say, where? And you say, The Up There. And I say, Up There? And you say, yeah, Up There. I say, where's up there? And you say, Yeah, The Up There.'

"It was a good time. Still is," Buzz finished, smiling at his comrades at the bar who had enjoyed portions of the story.

"Have one on me, you old *F.A.R.T.S.*," Dave said to Buzz.

"I'm ready," Buzz said.

Chapter Four
Peach Bowl Game

Before long, Saturday evening rolled around, and the Peach Bowl was upon them. Gary's promise of the spectacular box for the game had come true. *F.A.R.T.S.* young and old had assembled in their privileged spot inside the Georgia Dome to enjoy Southeastern Conference's University of Tennessee against the Atlantic Coast Conference's Georgia Tech. ESPN carried the event over 87,000 heads, live in the stadium.

The *ettes* had also arrived with or without guests, ready to enjoy every minute of the event—game, entertainment, and courtesy beverage service, too.

By halftime, things had started to slow down a little.

"Wooee! Look at this!" Bob Arnold called, squinting through binoculars. "You don't wanna miss this, McBride."

"You keep those things, Arnold. I'm seeing just what I want to see." Jack had secured himself a front row seat in the box, intent on catching every minute of every play.

Meanwhile, Dave took a seat at the bar, intent on catching every opportunity for a fresh drink.

"This is getting a little old," Fitz said, startling everyone. "Well," she said defensively with all eyes on her, "it *is!* Why don't they do something?"

The frustration was taking its toll. Las Vegas had laid a spread fourteen points in Georgia Tech's favor—but it looked as though somebody had forgotten to tell the members of the Tennessee team. Going out at halftime, Tennessee was up on Georgia Tech thirty-five to nothing.

"And if I hear that damned Rocky Top one more time, I think I'll start throwing some rocky tops," Fitz continued.

Every time Tennessee was in a position to make a down, kick-off, or score, their pep band would render its rough version of the aging Rocky Top tune, laying fuel on the fire, but never quite rallying the Georgia Tech troops to action.

But behind the scenes, something was about to take shape. Up in the Curtis box, *The Ghost* had been tapped into the Georgia Tech coach's headset all during the first half. This ghost had been silent, but he could feel the frustration on the part of the Coach MacDuff. Even when the disgruntled team headed for the showers at the half, he continued to listen. The assistant coach, still wearing his boss's headset, relayed a message to Coach MacDuff as he sat there, unable to find the words to rally his team.

"Coach," said the assistant, "the ghost would like a private word with you. He removed the headset from his sweaty dome and handed it to the coach.

The coach said nothing, retreated quietly into his private office.

Over his headset, the coach heard the thoughts of *The Ghost.* "It's time for something drastic, coach!" came the voice. "Here's a little something for ya. In 1957, when Bobby Dodd was up against Notre Dame, this is what they did…"

"What's he doin'?" Fitz asked, gesturing toward the front of the box. "Talkin' to himself?"

Buzz laughed. "I don't think so. I think he's got some tricks up his sleeve for the coach."

Fitz shook her head. "That guy's amazing," she said.

"How about another?" Dave said to Buzz. "You haven't had your quota yet."

"Oh, yes, I have!" laughed Buzz. "I know my limit!"

"And we're only at the half!" Dave said. "How are you gonna make it through?"

"I'll just have to get high on the game," Buzz answered.

"Well," Bob piped up, "everybody loves a challenge."

The group laughed. The football games were fun in *F.A.R.T.S.* territory. Not much more than excitement and good times rode on the outcome—and sometimes by the time the game was over, it didn't matter whether Tech had won or lost. The main thing was that they had played the game.

McBride called to the group. "They're getting ready for the kick-off," he said. "Shut up over there."

Before long, it was clear that MacDuff had taken the advice of the Ghost to heart.

"What is this shit?" demanded Harry, half disgusted, half amused.

"Just watch the game," McBride said. "And shut up."

"What is it, a midgets convention?" Mike asked.

"I think I'll have another," Dave said.

George Tech's team appeared to have gone through a shrinking machine—in fact, none of the players were even recognizable members of the team. There were twelve—all were scrub, third and fourth stringers, getting their first shot at big time ball. They were obviously undersized—in the kick-off, it looked as the first grade had challenged the eighth grade. They were doing just about as well, too.

Maggie had come with Harry, and as she sat sipping her spritzer, the scene struck her funny. At first she only giggled, but then, she broke into whole-hearted laughter. Before long, Harry, too, found the whole scene absurd. "It's like watching the munchkins versus the Munsters," he said, coughing at the same time.

"No," Gary said, "more like Bambi meets Godzilla…"

"All right, all right," said McBride. "A guy can't hear in here!"

Fitz looked over at Dave. "What's he talking about?" she asked.

"Look at him," Dave answered. "See that headset?"

Fitz nodded. "OK, so?"

"He ain't just listening. Our man McBride's got some history in his years. My guess is he's playing the Ghost again—telling MacDuff a thing or two about the old days."

"No shit!" Harry said. "What's he tellin' him?"

"If you'd shut up, you could watch it!" McBride called from across the room.

The laughing continued, but it was muffled, and mixed with newly emerging intrigue.

Tennessee started out the third quarter with a kick-off to Tech, who returned the ball to their twenty-five yard line. McBride raised the mike holder on his headset, "OK, I think you wanna fake one to the outside, coach," he said. "Tell your man Goldberg to do his act."

MacDuff was acting on blind faith. Whatever "his act" was, Goldberg could lay an egg as far as he was concerned. The play was conveyed to the field.

On the first snap, Goldberg was knocked down way out. He just lay on the ground like a sack of rotted potatoes. The same defender that hit Goldberg then moved center and pushed back the quarterback five yards. After the play, the defensive back returned to Goldberg, still laying flat on the ground, and helped him up. Goldberg sprung right up. It was comical to the onlookers, and laughter even jostled the shoulders of the players in the huddle. The second down went much the same way, ending in another five-yard loss. The defensive player, feeling a little less amused, helped Goldberg to his feet once again. Then, on the third down, Goldberg went down as before, but as the defensive back headed toward center to nail the quarterback, Goldberg jumped to his feet and ran like a jackrabbit down the sidelines. The quarterback, not heavily or even seriously pursued at that point, was easily able to lay a perfect shot into

Goldberg's hands. Goldberg carried the entire eighty-five yards untouched, for Georgia Tech's first touchdown of the game. Larry Travis's extra point brought the score to 35-7, Tennessee.

With the crowd screaming and laughing all at the same time, things were getting loud, both on the field and in the *F.A.R.T.S.* box.

"MacDuff!" shouted McBride, "get the kicker—get Travis!"

The coach raised his hand, and shook his head, not hearing.

McBride tried again. "Travis!" he shouted. "Tell Travis to do his backward shuttle!"

Again, having no clue, MacDuff stepped over to Travis, practicing for the kick-off. "Say, Larry," he said. "I think this would be a good time for that backward shuttle."

Larry's head jerked up and his eyes narrowed. "Is that you, Coach?" he asked.

MacDuff shook his head. "Hey, look, I'm doing a consult here. Do you know any backward shuttle?"

"I sure do!" Travis responded. "I'd be honored!" The young kicker made the rounds quickly with the kick-off team. "Backward shuttle," he said, a grin on his face.

"You got it, Trav," came the responses.

Minutes later, the ball was on the tee. Travis moved back into position, then shuttled back some more, and then rushed backward, hitting the ball with his heel. With all the guys ready, Tech's recovery was in the bag. They got it at their forty-five yard line.

"Tech's ball!" came the call.

The crowd went wild.

"I told you I'd get high on the game," Buzz called over to Dave.

"I believe you!" Dave said.

"Try the spread out!" McBride shouted into his mike. "The spread out play!"

On the first down, everyone but the guards and the quarterback headed hard for the sidelines. The snap was good, and the center stepped up to block for the quarterback. The guards pulled in and gave him plenty of breathing room in the pocket. But instead of backing to throw, the quarterback jetted straight up the middle, and gently touched the ball on the ground in the end zone. Score!

"OK!" McBride called. "That's the way to deal with these Rocky Top nuts!"

Instead of kicking, they went for the two-pointer. Goldberg made a perfect catch, setting the score up to 35-15, Tennessee. And it was only the beginning.

At that point, the scrubs, having rescued their team from certain death, were rewarded with a break. Their teammates, unleashed from the locker room, hit the field like a pack of wild animals. The first stringers were so charged up you couldn't beat them with a baseball bat.

In all, Tech scored five more times in that half, bringing the final score to 35-50, Georgia Tech.

"You're the man of the hour!" Dave said, toasting Jack McBride.

"How do you know all this stuff?" asked Gary. "You guys are just full of surprises!"

"He's the Ghost," Dave answered for him, referring to McBride's secret high-tech rig. "He's been around this stadium a long time. And he's got a little help from the telescope on his balcony," he laughed. "Look at him! He's got the moves of twenty-two teams in his brain. I guess he just pulled out a good one for tonight."

"A great one," Harry said. "Hats off to Jack!"

"Hey, I don't mind being the man of the hour," McBride said, chuckling. "But you fellows will excuse me, won't you? I've just been summoned via headset here by Coach MacDuff himself. He would like the pleasure of my company at the locker room celebration."

"Oh, OK. Too much for the likes of us, now," Bob teased. "You gotta find yourself appropriately placed company…"

"You said it," Jack teased. "Guys with my talent kinda tend to flock together."

"Yeah, flock is right," Dave said. "Like a bunch of cuckoo birds."

McBride laughed out loud. "I'll save some of my fine self for you guys," he promised. "If I don't get drafted onto the team, that is."

With that, he exited the box. His presence was missed, but the party went on. After midnight, the bartender proclaimed that Dave had consumed the Dome record for beers at one game. An hour later, the Super Dome was empty, but the party in the Curtis box was still in full swing.

Chapter Five
Seniors on Campus

The outcome of the game and the merriment afterward was a high point in *F.A.R.T.S.* history. The story grew and details became more and more exaggerated with time, but life went on.

Marvin Lemons, who had a part-time assignment in the stadium as chief of security, enjoyed his association with McBride, "the guy in MacDuff's ear," in the games that followed. And although not all went quite as spectacularly, it was a blast for the retired cop.

His reputation had grown so that he found himself invited—for a respectable fee—to give a semi-annual talk on self-defense and protection to the members of the inter-sorority council. His extensive experience lent him easy access to the most common means and methods of attack. He took it from there.

"So what are you gonna do, Maryanne, if the guy is hanging around in the parking lot? Say you're halfway from the door and your car, but he's closer to your car. What do you do?"

"I run like hell back to the door!" Maryanne answered, feeling a chill.

"Right! And Shelly, what if you didn't see the sonofabitch until you get to your car and he tries to get your keys and force you into the car. What do you do?"

"Get away, right?"

Everybody laughed. "Yeah, that would be a good plan," Marvin said, shaking his head. "But what if he's holding a gun on you? Shouldn't you just do as he says?"

"No," she said steadily. "You chance it and run. If he gets you in the car, you're dead anyway."

"Right!" Marvin smiled. There hadn't been any fatal incidents on campus that semester, and it boded well with him to be contributory in any part of it.

As life progressed for Marvin Lemons, so it did for the Ghost, Jack McBride. Although he held no official title, he lent out his services in a manner that suited him—unofficially—in just about sport the university offered. He had become a regular fixture in the summer basketball camp, which was held on Georgia Tech's campus.

Schwelfer, too, had a gift he was kind enough to share with the Tech students.

"You really a Kappa Sig?" Gary asked him one day as they walked along.

"Yeah, I'm Kappa Sig—University of Delaware, right over the Maryland line in Newark, Delaware. Good old school. Small, but good."

"Well, listen, if you're really a brother, maybe you could help us out, Dave," Gary went on.

"Whatever you need!" Dave said in earnest. "You just let me know!"

"Well, it goes like this…" Gary said, a smile creeping across his face.

And that was how it came to be that Kappa Sig Dave Schwelfer, class of '50, was entrusted with the title of Chief Keg Tester. He took his duties seriously, and quite liberally. Often, he would spend hours making sure the beer was the right taste, bouquet, and temperature. It was widely understood that Dave Schwelfer appreciated his job as much as those he served appreciated him.

It was only Bob Arnold who actually remained in business—to a certain extent. But he had conceived of an ingenious manner in which to combine his part time business with his one true love—observation of the female body. What better place for the discreet set of eyes than a college campus in the temperate zone? Without a terribly demanding schedule, Bob was able to enjoy this sport from his very favorite spot—a bench on campus in a park only a few hundred yards from his apartment. It was generously shaded most of the year by an old poplar tree. His bench faced North Avenue, but to the right was the favored Janie Swann Dorm, which housed over two hundred female coeds. It was an ideal location, as behind him lay the campus administration building, and to his left, Bobby Dodd stadium. Traffic was glorious—and fully appreciated.

The private side of Bob held an even deeper appreciation for the location. There, at the sidelines of Major Peter Pitman Park, he was in clear view of fallen Vietnam War Hero's memorial dedication. Major Pitman had graduated Georgia Tech, then, only months later, been killed in action in the summer of 1967. Arnold had come to feel as though both he and Major Pete owned the land. His respect for the war hero's sacrifice drove him to maintain the park, keeping it not only clear of litter, but also fragrant and lush with flora. He polished the bronze of the memorial plaque. In fact, he even carried on candid conversations with the major.

"Hah! Pete, get a look at those lovelies," he'd say as a group of especially attractive students happened by out of earshot. "You ever get anything that nice while you were hanging around here?"

Bob wasn't batty. He didn't expect to get any answers. But being ex-military himself, he had high respect for the fallen hero. Spending time at his memorial gave him a warm and homey feeling that he'd long lost any remnant of in his small apartment. Once Cecelia had died, the apartment had been a place to live and run the small business. His real life went on in the park—and at the Yellow Jacket Bar.

"Hi Bob," came one of the regulars as she passed him. "Great day for sunbathing!" In her tone was just a hint of a flirt.

"Yes, indeed!" Bob called back to her. "It's very healthy, a little sun."

The girl and her companion giggled.

"I think he's checking out your legs!" her friend said.

"He wouldn't be checking out my legs," the girl called over her shoulder, loudly for Bob to catch. "Legs are not his thing."

They moved on, as Bob sat there wondering, how in the world do they know I'm an upper body connoisseur? "Even the young ones can read your mind, Pete," he said. "Good thing you got out when you did. No disrespect intended."

It wasn't too long before a few of the young ladies from Janie Swann dormitory set up their blankets, laid down, and began spreading on suntan oil. Bob took it all in. Then he noticed others taking it in as well, but pushing a little further than was appreciated by the young beauties.

"Are you girls from Janie Swann?" a fellow student asked.

When no one answered, he tried again. "Hey, don't you all live at Janie Swann, over there?" He indicated with his finger poking the air in the direction of the dorm.

"No offense, but we're trying to get a little sun without the guys," one of the girls spoke up.

The young man appeared to have taken her remark as an invitation. He sat down next to her. "Yeah, isn't it great, being out here on a day like this?"

The first girl responded by moving away from him. Another reiterated the message of the first. "Listen, we're all for socializing at the parties and wherever else, but we're not into getting picked up while we're sunbathing, OK?" She was pleasant enough, but the fellow didn't seem to get the message.

Out of nowhere, the young man heard a voice. "Hi Beth, how are things going in Black Belt class? I heard you just about destroyed the instructor last class?"

"Oh, you wouldn't believe it," the girl answered. "I missed one of the kicks and it hit him right where you know where! He just about fainted."

The young man rose instinctively, his hand inadvertently covering his crotch.

"Well, I'll see you," he said faintly against the continued conversation between Bob and Beth.

"Well, I sure hope he doesn't try to get even," Bob laughed. "He'd just be in for more trouble after school."

The girls laughed.

"She really knows how to hurt a guy," one girl said.

"Yeah, Beth is a real ball breaker," said another.

They laughed hysterically. When the boy was gone from sight, the one Bob had been addressing as Beth said, "Thanks, Bob, you're the best!"

"Glad to help, Elissa," he said. "You ladies make it a pleasure."

They giggled appreciatively as he returned to his bench to read the paper, and enjoy the sights around him. He thought of what he had to do at home.

Bob had always known baking, but in retirement, he'd started his own cottage industry by sending out flyers to all he could think of, advertising his personalized cake baking service for birthdays and special events. His was a nice side business, and he truly enjoyed it. Eventually, he had secured the addresses of all of the out-of-town students' parents. With this information, he matched up a nice brochure, suggesting to the parent that he or she order a birthday cake for their child which would be delivered directly. He had a bare minimum of four one week, and a high of twenty-seven. That was a lot of baking. His expertise, however, had made him even more appreciated than simply the grounds keeper of Major Pittman Park.

But one day, the tables were turned on him. He would never know how the girls had learned the date of his birthday. But on that day, May second, he found himself surrounded by a group of twenty women.

"Ladies, take it easy on me," he teased. "I'm seventy years old, for crying out loud."

They giggled. Then, fifteen of them tightened ranks into a semi-circle facing him. The other five held their blankets high behind and beside him.

"What in the world?" Bob asked, completely confounded.

Just then, the girls turned away, loosened their tops, and then joined arms as they turned to face the birthday boy. Fifteen pairs of bouncy, coed breasts smiled happily at the old fellow.

Bob Arnold's eyes flew open wide. "Did I die?" he asked. "Is this heaven?" It was all he could say, over and over, as the girls stood there, arms linked together, motherly love taking in the scenery. "Happy Birthday to you," they sang, moving to the rhythm, "happy birthday to you. Happy Birthday, dear Bob, Happy Birthday to you."

Bob wanted to say that no cake could take the place of that sight, but all he kept repeating was, "Did I die? Is this heaven?"

Chapter Six
Meetings

The *F.A.R.T.S.* were not timid about meeting outside of the Yellow Jacket Bar. In fact, they had scheduled prayer meetings three times a month. Of course, when you're a *F.A.R.T.S.* member, the meaning of such an encounter takes on quite a different tone.

The meetings started out traditionally. A sign was tacked to Jack McBride's number 1702 apartment or Bob Arnold's, at number 815, that said:

Farternity Among Retirees & Tech Students
Prayer Meeting
DO NOT DISTURB.

Members assembled peaceably, often carrying things in brown paper bags that could have been Bibles and prayer books or other devotional materials. They were greeted affectionately at the open door, and ushered in. When the entire group came to order, the door was closed, signifying the beginning of the event.

"Come to order, please," Harry Thomas began. As the members settled down and found seats around the table, he continued, "Mr. Lemons, will you please lead us in a word of prayer?"

Everyone solemnly lowered his head, hands in the lap, eyes cast down.

Marvin Lemons rose, looked up to the ceiling, shook his head slightly, and uttered fervently, "God is good."

He then sat back down.

"I would like to thank you, Marvin, for those most inspiring words," said Harry.

Dave rose and said, "I make the motion to end the meeting."

Harry acquiesced. "All in favor, say 'ay.'" Without waiting even a millisecond for a response, Harry proclaimed, "The ays have it. Meeting adjourned."

"Let the games begin!" Joe Jenkins shouted. "Who's got the cards?"

And the group immediately mobilized, extracting chilled six packs and containers of martinis from their bags, and filling the table with chips and snacks of all kinds. Dave took out a bundle wrapped in waxed paper. He opened it and laid it on the table beside the rest.

"What the hell is that?" asked Bob.

"Why, that's Philly pretzels," Dave answered. "Haven't you ever seen 'em before?"

"Well, being that I'm not from Philly…"

"Nah, you don't have to be from Philly…"

"I heard of Philly pretzels," Mike cut in. "Let me try one. They're supposed to be kinda doughy, right?"

"Doughy? What kinda pretzel is doughy?" Bob demanded. "A pretzel should be hard, crunchy. Has it got any salt, for crying out loud?"

"Yeah, it's got salt!" Jack said, offended. "It's got the good kind. Look at 'em. It's the cubed kind, you know, looks like little squares."

"Oh, you mean rock salt," said Gary. "Yeah, I know what you're talking about now. I got some of those you put in the toaster oven over school."

"You don't put these in the toaster oven," Jack said. "They're Philly pretzels!"

"You're thinking of Dutch pretzels, Gary," Buzz said. "From your frozen foods department."

Marvin laughed. "OK, OK, Philly pretzels. I'm sure they're fine, after all, we've had our prayer and they were blessed along with all the rest of this high cholesterol stuff. Let's get the game going!"

The prayer meetings were just as often held in Bob Arnold's apartment, number 815. One night, before the prayer portion of the meeting, but after the sign had been tacked up and the outer door closed, Bob took Gary aside.

"Listen, Gar," he said, "you seem like the sleuthing type. Let me ask you something. How come every time I come in or go out of this apartment, I hear the apartment door of my next door neighbor open, then quickly close? It's an old gal in there, by herself, I think."

"She might be some nosey old woman with nothing to do but follow you around," Gary said.

"You think she's hot for me?" Bob asked, his eyebrows raising.

Gary laughed. "Hey," he said, "you got a set of golf clubs?"

"Sure. Over in the closet, there."

Gary extracted the ball retriever and closed the closet door. "How about some tape and a nice round mirror?"

"Sure."

"Come on out to the balcony with me," Gary said. "Let's bring the stuff." After Gary had finished, Bob had his own personal neighbor-watcher, with the mirror secured to the wide end of the ball retriever, which, if angled correctly, gave an excellent view of the woman in question. At that particular moment, she stood stock still at the wall dividing the two apartments. A suspicious drinking glass made contact with the wall and her ear simultaneously.

Gary burst out laughing. Bob had to send him back inside. But he stayed out a while, just to see how long the woman would hold her position. After five minutes in the chilly January night, he gave up and went inside.

"What's that all about?" he asked Gary, who was busy conceiving a plan with Buzz.

"Maybe you're right, Bob," Gary said. "Maybe she's hot for you."

"You think so?"

"Listen, tomorrow night, here's what you do..."

The very next night, with Gary, Buzz, Marvin and Dave arriving silently to covertly enjoy the event, Bob Arnold entered his apartment with an attractive, college-aged girl. Just as he approached his door, Bob heard the familiar quiet opening of the door at his neighbor, number 813's, residence. After he and his "date" stepped inside, it closed. For a few moments, Bob and the girl made smalltalk, laughing—which was easy to do under the circumstances—and trying to sound romantic. Gary signaled from the deck that old number 813 was securely at her post, glass raised, ear attached.

"Do you mind if I take off your blouse?" Bob said to the wall against which the old woman was listening.

"Here, let me help you," answered the girl. "It's tricky."

After a moment, Bob said, "Ah...those are magnificent!"

"Thank you," the girl said, giggling.

For a while, the two did loud impressions of marathon runners at their twenty-first mile, puffing and panting, and even throwing in some groaning. Donna Summer would have been jealous. Then, Bob's partner got a little creative.

"Oh Boner! Yes! Yes! Oh Boner!" she called. She carried on for a long while, with some of the guys there for the humor exchanging bewildered glances, and trying to disengage from the moment.

With one final screeching, "Boner!" the girl started laughing silently, along with Bob, who was as mystified as anyone, but grateful for the new nickname.

"That was terrific, Baby," he said to the wall.

"Oh, you know it! Can I come back tomorrow—I've got two friends who really need to meet you," she said.

As they left, number 813 failed to pursue her surveillance. "Gee, I hope she's all right," Bob said to Gary.

The next night, Bob returned to his apartment at the same time—and with three women.

His own surveillance team was already in place, ball retriever extended and ready for observation.

"Bob," Gary said, "you're not going to believe this. You gotta see this!"

Bob and the girls carefully stepped out onto the balcony. There, in the old woman's apartment, stood no less than eight, hefty, very intent women, ready for the show. Five held their heads up to glasses against the one wall, one used a toilet paper roll with waxed paper on the end, and two had stethoscopes!

The four actors commenced the routine, wild with lusty passion, and peppered with deep moans for the infamous "Boner." Alternately the actors took turns on the balcony, struggling to stay in character against the backdrop of what they witnessed in the next apartment.

For not one second, by all accounts, did a single woman lift her head from her listening device. Some were deeply mesmerized, others uttered inaudible expressions to themselves. One larger woman in a purple taffeta dress kept chanting, "Amen, Brother! Amen, Brother!"

"Is she praising him, or praying for the salvation of his rotten soul?" Gary asked Marvin.

"Why you askin' me?" Marvin laughed.

Another woman continually crossed herself in a prayerful and contrite manner, not, however, losing an instant of the drama enacted through her glass against the wall.

Before long, some of the audibles were emanating from number 813. One of the more sophisticated eavesdroppers, one sporting a stethoscope, moved forward and backward to the rhythm of what she heard, her exceptionally round hips gyrating in such a manner as to suggest she'd enjoyed such pleasures years before.

"Why do they keep calling him *Boner*?" the one with the toilet paper tube asked.

"Is it Boner?" her friend answered. "I thought it was *Rover* they were saying."

"Oh, no, it's Boner, all right," number 813 spoke up. "I heard it last night. Boner this, Boner that."

"So why are they calling him that?" the first one asked again.

The rounded woman with the stethoscope paused in her pleasure for a moment to enlighten her lesser sisters. "Boner," she said, "is an erection. The man's got an erection."

"Yeah...but...so they're actually talking to...*it?*" the woman asked.

"If I knew one like that, *I'd* sure talk to it!" rounded hips responded, and quickly replaced her earpieces.

"Vince never called it *Boner*," chimed in one of the glass listeners. "He was always going, 'The Big Guy' this and 'The Big Guy' that, and always poking me with it, like it had a mind of its own."

"Sounds like it did!" laughed the toilet paper tube. She replaced her listening device against her spot on the wall so as not to miss any more of the informative performance.

The following morning, by ten o'clock, the gossip chain had worked so quickly that a line of fifteen college-aged—and misinformed—girls, waited outside Bob's apartment. It was a sad moment indeed for the old man, when he, feeling compelled toward honesty, had to decline the copious pleasures of the women so available to him. He did give each a special thank you hug, holding onto the chestier specimens just a little longer than required.

Later that afternoon as Bob rode down on the elevator, on his way to the bar, he witnessed the conversation between two of the upper floor residents who had not had the pleasure of membership in the eight-woman surveillance team of the night before.

"Oh good Lord! And I don't think I want to hear anymore about it. Right now anyway," laughed the woman. "They say it was a man named Mr. Boner."

"No, it must be Bonner, you know, old Mr. Bonner up on tenth. He's a black fellow."

"You said it. Ain't no white man in this building *that* talented."

Bob practiced his poker face, enjoying the infamy. Stepping off the elevator, he drew the attention of the usual hanger-outers in the lobby.

"There he is!" called one of them.

Spontaneous applause broke out as he proudly strutted through the small crowd. After traveling the short distance to the Yellow Jacket, Bob was greeted with a standing ovation by everyone inside the bar, and the inauguration of the ritual chant of, "Boner! Boner! Boner!"

Chapter Seven
Steeplechase
-or-
The Definitive Case Of Pressed Ham

In Atlanta, one of the true rites of spring is the Atlanta Steeplechase Races. On the first Saturday in April, over twenty-five thousand elite members of the yuppie set descend upon a small farm community north of the city. They assemble in order to witness the beautiful parade of thoroughbreds as they race over hill and dale, jumping fences along the way. The elite spectators are typically decked out in fancy attire, with many of the women showing in perfect long, flowing dresses, and wearing wide-brimmed sunbonnets, as if to claim, if only for the day, that singular part of the south their heritage.

The posh affair is further marked by the stunning displays in the infield of the finest table settings, in the company of beautiful floral arrangements in lead crystal vases, flanked by fine, polished, silver candlesticks and linen table dressings.

For the group from North Avenue, the day started at 9:00 am at the Yellow Jacket Bar with the obligatory Bloody Marys and Mimosas. For Sue Ecclestone, the co-owner of the establishment, it was a big moment. She took great pains to arrange every detail of the group's annual pilgrimage to the gala event, including the chartering of a bus that would shuttle the regulars to the Atlanta Steeplechase in style. She supervised the drinks, and most spectacularly, the sumptuous buffet for all of her passengers.

"You got them blintzes again, Sue?" Marvin asked as the group reached the steeplechase grounds.

"I got it all, Marvin!" Sue called.

"Tell it like it is, Suzy!" Bob shot out.

"Don't blame him," Buzz said, looking at her husband, Tim. "He's half-crocked already, and he couldn't help himself even if he weren't."

"Yeah, Boner, we know all about you," Tex called out.

And the chanting began. "Boner, Boner, Boner!"

"Shush!" Sue called out. "You're gonna get us kicked out before we get in!"

Harry and Maggie, the twenty-one-year-old Tech *ette* had sequestered themselves during most of the ride up.

"What are you two doing over there?" Jack McBride called. "Talking about sports?"

Everyone laughed.

"Just keeping current," Harry answered.

"Speaking of which," Mike said, "come on, Bob, let's take the numbers and stuff."

"All right. Who do you like for the first one, Schwelfer?"

"Let's see, they got this 'A's The Man,' looks like a good bet."

"Nah," Gary argued, "he started out OK, but he's getting kind of sluggish."

"I agree," Mike said. "'Johnny's Knight' looks right to me."

"You take 'im," said Dave. "I'll stick with 'A's The Man' and all that cash!"

Fitz picked up a copy of the form. "What is it, five bucks a race?"

"That's right," said Bob, "the winners of each race split the pot."

"Fair enough," she said, and joined the other ladies.

"You guys comin' in?" Harry said to Maggie.

"Yeah," she said. "Sure. Why not?" She leaned over toward Fitz to take a look. "What color's the A guy wearing?"

Fitz concentrated. "Hmm, I think it's red and white."

"What *color?*" Harry said. "Did you ask what color the jockey's wearing?"

"Yeah," Maggie answered. "So what?"

Most of the men had a good laugh.

"Anybody in stripes, today?" Jack called out, his voice noticeably higher.

"I'd like some poka dots and candy canes," Harry joined in, his most feminine voice."

"Shut up, Harry," Maggie said scowling and joining the ladies.

"Yeah, shut up, Harry," Charlotte joined in. "You guys have no clue."

"OK, OK," he said, throwing up his hands. "You bet on colors. It might teach you a few things."

"Yeah, it might," Fitz said. "Marta, here, you and Charlotte take a look at this one. I'll share with Maggie."

After the bets were all settled and recorded, the group enjoyed Sue's magnificent buffet and took in the races the best they could. By the end of the day, Marta had won fifty dollars, Maggie and Charlotte ninety each, and Fitz had won one hundred and thirty dollars.

"So how much did you win again?" Fitz asked Bob.

"Shut up, Fitz," Bob answered good-naturedly.

"Yeah," Harry joined in, "shut up, Fitz."

"Don't talk like that to her," Maggie teased, "or I won't share my loot with you."

"I think she means it, Harry," Bob said.

With the food cleaned up and packed away and only the lone bus driver absent an evening cocktail, the bus gently pulled out toward the throng of vehicles congregating on the small back road, waiting to enter the interstate. What followed was a story that would live and be duly embellished as the participants saw fit, for years, in the Yellow Jacket Bar honorary Hall of Fame.

After the bus made its way onto the little road, it moved little more a quarter of a mile in fifteen minutes time. As it happened, Dave, Bob, Buzz, and Jack were seated to the rear of the bus, and fell victim to the foul sounds of honking of an impatient motorist.

"Does he think we're sitting here because we want to?" Dave asked sarcastically.

"He's just some idiot out-of-towner," Bob said. "Look at that. Arkansas license plates."

"Ignore him," Buzz said. "Can't be too bright—he's got a University of Georgia sticker on his windshield."

"Well that explains that," Bob answered.

The driver then honked again.

"Hey, ya mother!" Jack said lightly.

The four of them turned to give the evildoer the hairy eyeball. And to their surprise, the little varmint gave them the finger.

Buzz laughed out loud as they turned back around. "The guy's on something!" he said.

"I don't know about that," said Dave resolutely, "but that sonofabitch needs a brand new perspective of the Schwelfer moon."

"Oh shit, here we go," muttered Jack, shaking his head.

Dave's moon had a certain degree of notoriety. As a student, in that testy posture, he had earned himself a temporary suspension from the University of Delaware. As it happened, Dave had been visiting friends of his at Gettysburg College on the same weekend that then Speaker of the House, Sam Rayburn, had been playing host to a group of foreign dignitaries, taking them on a tour of the famed Gettysburg Battlefields. Right around that time, Dave felt the urge to make his nonverbal statement from the rear to a driver unrelated to the distinguished Rayburn, yet in close proximity. It was the mooner's distinct misfortune to have been a little slow on the uptake—unable to conceal the "evidence" as quickly as the Secret Service had been to seize upon it.

The event did little to dissuade Dave from continuing to practice his questionable method of communication. And on that day, in the back of the *F.A.R.T.S.* transport, Dave did not hesitate to press his point to the rear, establishing the legendary full-moon effect—not just a peek and run show. Satisfied with the duration of his statement, Dave then attempted to disengage himself from the rear window of the bus. It was there that the trouble started.

"Hey, Jack," he said, "give me a hand, will ya?"

Jack turned around, startled to see how far backward his friend had extended himself. "What are you doing?"

"What do you think I'm doing?" Dave demanded in a nasty tone. He shouldn't have done that.

"You don't have to be so touchy," Jack said. "Hey, Buzz, get a load of this. Hot shot with his famous moon—stuck at the windowpane."

Buzz and Bob turned around. "Holy shit!" Bob said. "What'd you do that for?"

Buzz started to give him a hand, laughing so hard he shook.

"Hold up, there, Buzz," Bob said. "I say we let him stay there a while. It'll teach him some manners."

"I'm with you," Jack said. "Who says you gotta expose yourself to every irate passenger, anyway?"

"Hey, Buzz! Come on buddy!" Dave pleaded.

"Sorry," Buzz managed to choke out between bouts of hysteria. "I gotta go with the majority!"

By that time, everyone on the bus had joined the throng at the back of the bus, and no one was forthcoming with any assistance. In fact, Fitz had an idea.

"Hey Sue," she said, "any chance we can get Mel up there to pull over on the side of the road? I think we all need to get a full exposure to this interplanetary connection."

As they pulled over, Marcia, Dave's wife, just sat, shaking her head, half smiling, half scowling. The bus emptied out quickly and all but one of the *F.A.R.T.S.*, *ettes,* and guests gathered to look at the full moon. In very quick order, many other vehicles decided to pull over and have a look as well. Before long, there was quite a throng at the scene, all under the stoic supervision of one-eyed Dave.

The gathering, excessive collection of vehicles, and loud laughter got the attention of the local police.

"Is there a problem?" one of the officers asked Bob.

"No, Sir," Bob answered seriously. "But I think there's something you need to see."

No one made any move to rescue Dave. Most stood around with their arms crossed, one hand under their chins, and nodded, as if assessing the value of a work of art. When the police officers arrived and saw what had been drawing the crowd, they spoke little, and smiled a lot.

"These guys are all right," Mike mumbled to Harry, who nodded.

One of the officers spoke into his radio. "Lieutenant," he said, "I'm afraid we have a situation on Saddlebrook Road."

"What's the problem, Torelli?" came back the female voice.

"If it's alright, I'd just as soon you check this out, Ma'am," he said, his voice giving away nothing.

Arriving on the scene, the lieutenant played along quite seriously, but exchanged furtive amused glances with the other officers.

It happened that in one of the cars that had pulled over sat Carmen, an attorney and a semi-regular at the Yellow Jacket. He popped out and after negotiating his fee of three beers and two cigars, he sprang into action.

He entered the bus and greeted Dave, who was beyond embarrassed. "Carmen! Thank God you're here! Get me out of here!"

"I'm afraid I can't do that, Dave, but I just wanted to let you know that I'm on the job. Right now, we're going to secure the scene."

With that, Carmen jumped back off the bus, borrowed a roll of yellow and black crime scene tape, and circled the affected area of the window, creating a mostly rounded shape, with a protrusion at the bottom.

"I've brought these fine officers on board with me," Carmen announced, returning to his client with Marcia and the officers. "Here's Officer Klein, Officer Torillo, and Lieutenant Meyer," Carmen said jovially.

"Nice to meet you," Dave said weakly.

"Officers, my client waives his right to the reading of his rights," Carmen said, as Dave listened in a state of mild panic and total confusion.

"I'm afraid we're going to have to cuff you, sir," said Lieutenant Meyer.

Carmen nodded.

"Oh! He was a track star in college," Marcia added enthusiastically.

"Uh…Marcia…" began Dave.

"In that case, I'd say we have cause to cuff his ankles as well," said Lieutenant Meyer.

"I would like to photograph the scene," Carmen said to Lieutenant Meyer.

"That would be acceptable to the police," she said, "providing you will supply copies of your material evidence to the police department."

"Absolutely, absolutely!" said Carmen. He began to take pictures inside the bus, which set off a storm of flashes outside the bus, possibly making Dave Schwelfer the most photographed rear agenda in the state of Georgia.

Officer Torillo took over. "Sir, I'm charging you with 719 of the Penal Code of Forsyth County under Section D, which covers the act of mooning under the auspices of both the indecent exposure act and cruel and unusual punishment statute."

"But your honor—oh, excuse me—officer!" Carmen cut in. "I beg to interject. This case is not about mooning, officer. This offense sits squarely under the Pressed Ham Exception. Technically, we do not have a moon. If any portion of the buttocks or rear posterior area thereof shall be borne down upon, resulting in the clear and present compaction—without projectile—against the rear windshield, the act shall be construed as involuntary under the Pressed Ham Exception—of 1993, I believe."

"I respect your opinion, counselor," said Officer Torillo, "but I'll have to defer to Lieutenant Meyer."

"I could be convinced. Do you have evidence of the compaction, counselor?" Lieutenant Meyer asked.

"Please. Follow me," Carmen answered, as he led the parade back outside to the rear of the vehicle. "See here?" he said, indicating the areas touching the rear windshield by circling them with a magic marker. "These portions present us with an air-tight case."

"Let's hope it's airtight," Officer Torillo mumbled under his breath.

"I have to admit," said Lieutenant Meyer, waving a flashlight across the area Carmen had indicated, "this case does seem to butt right up against the Pressed Ham Exception of '93."

"Then I must insist that you release this man immediately," Carmen said dramatically as the crowd cheered and hooted. "Failure to do so will most certainly result in charges of falsifying ham."

"By all means. Torillo?"

"Do you want me to just take off the handcuffs, or do I have to detach him from the window, too?" Torillo asked in a pained voice.

"Use your own judgment, Officer," she answered, barely audible over the crowd.

By the following Monday, Buzz had produced a twenty-four by thirty-six-inch framed photo of the group outside the back ends of both the bus and Dave.

"I think you deserve this, my friend," he said to Dave, "just in case you ever have one of those days when you don't know which end is up."

To this day, Buzz's photo art holds a place of honor on the wall behind the bar at the Yellow Jacket Bar.

Chapter Eight
Buzz's Farewell

It was some weeks later, on a cool, damp Monday afternoon when the waitress summoned Dave for a phone call. In only moments, he returned to the bar, completely shaken. His eyes were glassy and he could not still the motion in his hands.

"Hey, what's up Dave? You all right?"

By then, several of the regular crowd had arrived.

Dave said in a voice very light, "Buzz died last night."

He took off his glasses and dragged a hand across his eyes. After he got his bearings a little better, he lifted his beer and headed for a booth in the far, unoccupied section of the bar. After a moment, he set his glasses down, rested his face in his hands and let loose a flood of emotions. His shoulders as the fear, dread, and sorrow of many months wracked its way through his being.

Sue Ecclestone did her best to comfort him. She'd seen the pair come and go together for almost three years. They had been closer than any of the others; almost as if they shared a common bond. Buzz was a mystery to all of them, but less so to Dave. And now, he's gone, she thought. What will the old fellow do?

"Come on, Dave," she said. "You gonna be OK?"

"I'll be all right," Dave said. But he could scarcely change his posture. "He was a good man," he managed.

"Oh, sure he was!" Sue said.

"No, I mean more than you know," he said. "He was something else."

"Look, I know you two were close," Sue said. "I know you've always been there for each other. But we're here for you now. You know, the rest of the group will always…" her voice cracked in mid-sentence as she happened to catch a glimpse of the famed Buzz in full Georgia Tech mascot dress. "I'm sorry," she said, as she, too, succumbed to emotion.

Within an hour, the booth was full and surrounded by the group.

"It was so sudden," Maggie said to Harry. "Wasn't it?"

"He seemed OK to me last week," Harry answered. "But…"

"He was sick," Dave said. "No, not that kind of sick. He had a heart condition."

Everyone nodded in understanding.

"It doesn't seem like the group," Marta said softly.

"It's still the group," Fitz answered. "We're just missing one and ten to one he's with us here, anyway. Probably laughing, too."

"He's probably thinkin' of Dave's pressed ham," Bob chuckled, trying to sooth his old buddy.

Dave just shook his head and smiled. He moved his mouth to say something, cleared his throat, and then shook his head some more, resting his temple on his hands.

Harry returned to the group from the bar. "I've spoken to someone at his house," he said. "There's going to be a viewing tomorrow night. It's at the family home just off West Paces Ferry, near the governor's mansion. Next day is the service at Christ the King Catholic Church on Peachtree Street. Dave, they've asked me to ask you to serve as pallbearer."

Dave nodded, closing his eyes.

Tim appeared, carrying a tray of Buzz's famous birdbath in and out martinis. "I hope this isn't inappropriate…"he began.

"No at all," Dave said. "Everyone, drink up. Let's toast our friend."

Theodore "Buzz" Anderson had held his hand close to the vest throughout their time together. He'd laughed and talked and lived just as heartily as all of the other *F.A.R.T.S.*, yet the details of his life had been sketchy. They knew some about his parents, whom he adored. But he'd never mentioned any siblings or extended family, other friends, or work at Coca Cola—and definitely nothing about Vietnam. That was a chapter that had been sealed and sunk—something locked tightly in the back of his mind.

"I think we should all go to the services," Fitz said, breaking the growing silence. "It would be horrible for the parents if nobody showed up—I mean nobody but us."

"You're right," Sue agreed. "Why don't we all meet here tomorrow. Six o'clock. All right?"

"That's fine, that's fine," said Dave, wiping his nose. "Now I've got to get out of here and look for my good suit…"

One by one, except Harry and Maggie, who left together, the group dispersed, thinking gentle thoughts of their fallen *F.A.R.T.S*.

At the antebellum mansion the next day, no one said a word as they were guided by police personnel to parking areas and politely shown the waiting line that stretched a full two hundred yards down the walkway.

After a time, Fitz muttered to Charlotte, "And I thought maybe no one but us would show."

Charlotte giggled. "I guess we don't know as much as we think we do."

In time, they were greeted by Theodore Anderson, Sr. The older man, who looked to be in his middle seventies, was completely composed and greeted them very warmly. "Oh!" he said when Fitz introduced them, "you're the *F.A.R.T.S.!* How lovely to meet you!" He turned to his left and said enthusiastically to his wife, "Ingrid, Ted's *F.A.R.T.S.* are here!"

"Oh my!" said the equally lovely woman. And she hugged each of them affectionately. "I'm so happy to know you. We have heard, as I'm sure you imagine, quite a lot about your activities with Teddy."

"It's a pleasure to meet you," Fitz said, followed by the others.

"I would like all of you to meet a dear family friend since 1949," Ingrid said. "This is Monsignor Keirnan. In fact, he'll be saying the funeral mass tomorrow. Monsignor, these are Teddy's friends from North Avenue."

Monsignor lit up like a Christmas tree. "Ah! The *F.A.R.T.S.* and the fartettes!" he exclaimed lightly, keeping his voice low.

While Mrs. Anderson returned to greet the line of visitors, the line of which had grown beyond three hundred yards down the walk, Monsignor spoke to the group. "I feel as though I've known all of you over the past few years," he said. "Ted has talked about you all every week at Sunday dinners, telling us about your adventures. The happiness—the true joy in his voice—meant so very much to his mother and father," he said.

"That's great to hear," Harry said. "You know, but, we only knew him down on North Avenue—just while he was there. We never really got to know as much of him as we'd like to have, although he talked a lot about his parents."

The monsignor smiled. "Yes," he said, as if remembering something from long before. "You probably don't know that he was quite a war hero. He saved many many lives in Vietnam. He received more commendations in his four years of service than many officers do in a career."

As they moved along to view the body of their friend, Maggie spoke for all of their feelings. "I think Buzz was a lot more than we imagined," she said. "I always thought he was a great guy, but I think he was much more than that—and to a lot of people."

The casket was situated in the room, Monsignor explained, that Buzz had loved best in their home. It was a kind of den on a grand scale. It was cleared of all furniture except for catered chairs and of course the casket, which sat on an onyx stand at the head of the room. The room held photos of the Anderson's beloved only child through all stages of his development, including pictures of his achievements in fourth grade soccer, other team sports, and his graduation from Georgia Tech. One photo that seemed oddly out of place amongst the others was that of an award ceremony. In it, President Nixon stood pinning an award for bravery to young Anderson's chest.

At each end of the casket, a military honor guard stood proudly at attention. Far off in a corner, observing but clearly alone in the crowd, stood two-star General James G. Bailey. Dave had never met the man, but he knew Army insignia, and he knew well of the man. He wandered over, with the others straggling behind.

"You must be Bailey," he said.

"Yes, sir, I am," Bailey answered.

"My name's Dave Schwelfer," Dave said. "I'm sorry for your loss."

"And I for yours, Mr. Schwelfer."

"You know of me?"

"Oh yes. I haven't seen Ted in eight years," he answered, "but we talked frequently on the phone. I surely knew of you—and I bet I know who the rest of these folks are." His tone warmed ever so slightly.

"I guess he spoke of us," Dave said smiling. "Was Ted under you?"

"Yes, he was an Army Ranger. I don't know if you know what that means in today's terms, but they play roles as individuals. They have no back-up, no team, no surveillance. They simply go on the mission, take care of the business, and

God-willing, they return to camp. They train alone, study alone, and then go out on duty alone. It's one of the toughest jobs in the military."

The others were silent, trying to imagine their jovial, well-dressed, clearly refined drinking buddy in such a capacity. The crowds had grown in the room, and they were glad to be in a far corner.

"Can you tell us any more about him?" Bob Arnold asked timidly.

"I can tell you that over the four years he was in I had twenty men assigned to me, and he was the top—he was the best of the best. Many nights he would go on missions—all of them behind the lines—gathering information, critical for us. The fellow had heart. I could see that from the beginning when he developed a specialty of retrieving American captives and seeking out downed pilots. Sometimes he'd be gone a week or two, but he'd always—and I mean *always*—get the job done. In his fourth year out there, he took command of his last mission. It was out on the Delta. An Air Force pilot had gone down. Ted spent three days along the Mekong River before he found his man. He got very sick. It was most likely Agent Orange, which was used heavily in that area. But he got his pilot and he got back. Trouble is, when he returned, he was so sick the stuff had gotten to his heart. 'You got a year to live,' the doctor's told him. Hey, you think that fellow Rambo is tough. He was nothing compared to Ted Anderson, Jr. That was thirty years ago!" The general's voice rose for the first time during the narrative. He composed himself, and continued. "See, if he shut you out of some of this, you have to understand, he didn't know when he'd be gone."

Dave wore a knowing look on his face.

"Sort of the way a police officer keeps the dangerous stuff away from his wife and family," Bailey went on. "But he'd have never gotten married—he couldn't see doing that to anybody. To my knowledge, there were only the six of us who knew about his heart condition; his mother and father, the monsignor, a fellow he knew from school named Bob Kiff that we call 'Pork,' Dave Schwelfer, here, and me. And as Mr. Schwelfer can tell ya, we were made to promise not to tell anyone.

"A funny thing is, and I can tell you this now. Ted's code name on operations was 'Buzz Man.'"

The listeners, eager to know about their lost friend, took it all in with a new depth of appreciation and respect for their friend—and with a measured amount of sorrow for not having been able to admire the man while he'd been alive with them.

At the funeral the following day, Jack said as much to Dave.

"But you know," Dave said, "it was his way. It was his choice. I mean we paled around a lot so I got to know things I might not have—but that was his way. He had no sense of ego. None at all. He went around letting everybody think he was gay, for gods' sakes."

"He wasn't?" Maggie asked.

"Nah," Dave said. "I've got stories. But later. I think they're getting ready to talk now."

The crowd pulled closely together with Mr. and Mrs. Anderson and Monsignor Kiernan at the center by the casket. As everyone focused on the monsignor, he said, "See that hill over there, out at the edge of this cemetery?"

Everyone focused just in time to see the Georgia Tech yellow jacket mascot waving his arms. Quickly then, it disappeared out of sight.

"Although Ted is out of our sight," Monsignor Kiernan went on, "his soul, his spirit lives on, and his memory in our hearts. I can just hear God saying to him, 'Theodore 'Buzz' Anderson, Jr., come on in! You're crispy, yes, that's it. You're crispy. Come on in!"

It was a bittersweet moment. There were no doubters at the funeral. Ted was with God, for all concerned, he was happy. But for the suddenness of his departure, and the new knowledge that he'd been only slightly known to them, the *F.A.R.T.S.* and *ettes* felt an empty, drilling sorrow.

Sue and Tim, hoping to help fill the void for all, invited everyone present to a reception at the Yellow Jacket following the burial service. They set up a fine buffet in a private dining room, and decorated it with Buzz's favorite flower—carnations. It was a flower he'd worn often in his lapel over the years in his ever-present suit, and a flower that had accompanied his body that afternoon. By 2:00 pm, the Yellow Jacket dining room was filled with a warm collection of Buzz's family, friends from the bar, high school, college, and even work at Coca Cola. In fact, during the course of the afternoon, even the president of Coca Cola, Kenneth Carlson, put in an appearance to express his loss and warm wishes to Buzz's friends.

Later that evening, as things thinned out, Dave found himself in the company of Bob Kiff. "Don't they call you 'Pork'?" he said.

"That's right," Pork answered. "And you're Schwelfer, right?"

"Yeah, bar buddy, I guess you'd say."

"I heard it was more an' that," Pork said.

"We were close, I guess."

"We were best friends from high school at Westminster and roomed together at Tech. He was the captain and top dog of gymnastics—and I held my own in baseball. We were some pair. He was a real guy, you know what I mean?" Pork said. "Somebody to look up to, but somebody to hang with, too."

"Mind if an old Army fart joins you two?" Bailey asked, approaching with a martini in hand.

"Well, in case you don't know it, this is the place for *F.A.R.T.S.*" Dave answered.

The other two chuckled. "Heard all about it," Bailey said.

"Yeah, yeah," Pork said. "Why don't we get a booth over there? I'm getting a little wobbly."

Once they'd sat down, Dave felt comfortable. "I feel like I share something with you guys, yet we've only just met."

"It's funny that way, isn't it?" Pork said. "Ted was like that."

"I think when I first learned about his real background was during an amazing experience I had with him walking right out there, just over Peachtree St.," Dave said.

"Go ahead, Schwelfer," Bailey said. "I'd like to hear it."

"Me, too," Pork said.

"Well, it was a little less than two years ago," Dave began, "and we were walking, like I said, down Peachtree. It must have been somewhere around 9:00 pm and this old Ford pulls up, jerks to a stop and four punks get out racin' for us. 'Give us your fuckin' money! Give us your fuckin' money, now!' one of them screamed, holding a gun to Ted's head.

"I was getting a little wired, there, having four thugs descend on us two, me up there and Ted, himself, near fifty. But he just plays cool as ice. He goes, 'Gentlemen! Gentlemen! Why don't you earn it?' And the screamer looses it for a second. He's confused. I think he was on crack, to tell you the truth. Anyway, the guy goes, 'What the fuck do you mean?'

"'Well,' Ted says, 'put the gun down. And then the four of you try to whip it out of me. But you gotta leave my associate alone."

"These guys were hot for the job, little cowards. 'Yeah, man, we haven't put a hurt on a fag in a couple of months,' he says. 'That sounds like a whole lotta fun!'

"So Ted looks at me and he says, 'Gentlemen, I am not gay. Dave, are you gay?' in that same sort of cool, James Bondy kinda way."

Pork and Bailey both laughed. "That's Ted," Bailey said.

"Anyway, of course I answered, no I'm not gay either, but it didn't matter what we said. Those four guys start dancing around Buzz real street like, and one of 'em pulls out a knife. And what does Buzz do, but lean back, exasperated, and say to these guys, 'I thought you wanted to put a hurt on me! What are you going to do? Dance me to death?"

"The mouthy one gets hot and moves right up in his face, and Buzz headbutted the guy—he broke his nose in three places—and of course he keels. Then he gets the next guy with a karate shot, I don't even remember where it was so fast, and he falls down like a sack of flour. Even before the second thug hit the turf, Buzz spun around so fast he caught number three—ow!—right in the nuts." Dave squinched up his face. "It was brutal. As the guy goes forward in pain, he nailed him again—this time a dropkick, right under the chin. The only one still standing is the guy with the knife. He couldn't do much, but I think he was trying to convince himself because he kept sort of jabbing at nothing and saying 'I'm gonna cut you bad! I'm gonna cut you bad!' While this guy is still holding the knife, his hand ends up behind himself and he must have felt a nasty puncture right in his ass. Buzz knocked him into the pile of losers, opened up the trunk of that old Ford and laid 'em all in there.

"Of course I'm standing there—the whole thing took less than a couple minutes. 'Did I just see what I think I saw?' I asked. Buzz just chuckled and said, 'The nerve of some people—calling me a fag! You know very well I'm crispy! This whole thing has definitely put me in the mood for an in and out.' We laughed. I said, 'I think I'll have a couple.'

"He made a nine-one-one call as we headed for this place, and said something along the lines that he'd heard some noises coming from the trunk of an old Ford on Peachtree and so on. That was when he started to let me in on how he knew how to take care of himself that way, and you know, little bits at a time, I guess. I was more honored to know him at that point, I'll tell you that.

"Anyway, we were still at the bar here when the evening news comes on. They got Action News, Channel Two, and this Monica Kaufman lady comes on. She goes, 'Police reportedly found four men locked in the trunk of a car on Peachtree Street near the Fox Theatre this evening.' Well we started laughing. They cut over to the on-the-scene guy, and it's live! The fellow says, 'Thank you, Monica. As you can see, the police have just opened the trunk of this 1989 Ford Fairlane, and removed four men. All of the men are alive and believed to be in their twenties. They have been beaten, and one is apparently suffering from a knife wound to the buttocks, but none of their injuries appear to be life-threatening. Police Lieutenant Malcomb says that one man reported that the four had been attacked by a gang of ten to fifteen men. However, the Lieutenant believes the four in the trunk are the same four who have been effectively terrorizing the midtown section of Atlanta. They have retrieved a weapon from the vehicle which matches the make and caliber of one used in the recent murder in Buckhead. Police say the four will be treated at Grady Hospital, and likely then taken into custody and charged with the incidents.'

"It was great. We were rolling on the floor. Of course Train there thought we'd lost it. I couldn't tell anybody what he'd done for me, and he wasn't going to either. I guess that was really the beginning of our stronger bond of friendship."

"That story don't surprise me in the least," Bailey said, sipping his martini.

"Me either," Pork said. "You'll love this one, too. Let me get another beer…"

"I'll get it. I need a refill myself," Dave answered.

Sue smiled at Tim. "I think we did a good thing, having this here," she said. "Look at Dave. He's with two of Buzz's closest friends."

"There's nothing like swapping war stories," Tim said. "But it's gonna take some time, you know."

"I know. Oh, he's getting up. I bet they're looking for a refill."

"Dave? What else does he want?" Tim laughed.

When the three had settled in again, Pork started his story. "You know Ted was the mascot over there, but you don't know that he was pressured into it. He felt stupid at first, running around in a bee outfit. But they didn't have anyone else, so he went on with it and in time, I think it was the fact that he could cause a stir that got him. Just running around as the mascot used to generate some flutter of activity. And when you combine what he could do as a gymnast—he was unstoppable. Of course he became the best mascot Georgia Tech ever had. And that caused him a little problem.

"The biggest deal at Georgia Tech for the jocks was that Thanksgiving morning freshman football game against the University of Georgia. There were over 30,000 fans, and the event was a charity thing. Helped raise money for the Scottish Rite Hospital there. Anyway, it was on a Thanksgiving game that Ted nailed his first back flip from across the bar. That became his trademark. And he really was a source of energy for the fans. They loved him. It made the team play better with all that glitter and excitement in the air.

"Well, that afternoon, as he's leaving the stadium, some jokers throw a blanket over him and kidnap him in a van to Tech's arch-rivals' campus about seventy miles away. They tied him up, but allowed him one phone call to his parents, to let them know he wasn't have Thanksgiving Dinner at home. Well, I guess his captors had a little too much turkey, or maybe something else, but they fell asleep. Buzz was a gymnast—it's hard to tie up a gymnast right. And he was no exception. He was outta there and to a phone booth in minutes. He had me pick him up there in Athens. 'Bring me a change of clothes,' he says. So when I get to

Athens in the middle of the night, I find a very hungry bee at the phone booth. 'You need some honey?' I teased him. He said, 'Don't you worry about that. Just give me the clothes. We're on a mission!' That's how in the middle of the night, I found myself heading for Savannah, the home of Uga, the University of Georgia's bulldog mascot. Ted told me to wait with the motor running and he'd be right back. He scaled that eight-foot fence like a monkey, up and back, even carrying a sixty-pound, fairly amiable dog. But I have to say that not only was it the ugliest thing I'd ever seen, it laid a trail of farts from Savannah to Atlanta, non-stop."

"Maybe that's where the theme started…" Dave chuckled.

"Yeah!" laughed Pork. "I guess he never forgot it! Anyway, it was early Friday morning by the time we got back. The next day, Saturday, back at Grant Field, we were set to have our traditional game against the University of Georgia. It was a sell-out crowd. But the Georgia guys were distraught and outraged at the disappearance of their famed mascot. It might have affected their play. With only a few seconds left on the clock, Georgia Tech's quarterback sent a bomb down the field, and they made a touchdown, kicked a good extra point and won that game in a millisecond, twenty-one to twenty. You can imagine the fans were going out of their minds. As we expected, they started chanting for Ted. They want to see that patented backflip. They're screaming and carrying on and he walks out onto the field with a knapsack on his back. He does the flip—perfectly, even with the knapsack. Now wait till you hear what's inside that knapsack! He opened it up and decked out in pink ribbons, out walked Uga."

"That's it, you know, that creative element," Dave said, his words slurring slightly. "That was Ted. Be correct, but be a little creative."

"Like a knife to the buttocks," Bailey chuckled.

"Yeah, right," Dave said.

"Well, I have to agree," Bailey said. "I've got one for you guys, too."

"By all means," said Pork.

"There's a lot to tell about the guy," Bailey began, "but I guess my favorite was his soldier retrieval story in broad daylight. The fact is, the soldier in captivity had lost two brothers in battle there, and he was the last one living. Ted carried the white flag, dressed in only underwear and his boots. He carried no weapons. It was a big camp, over ten thousand enemy were housed in it, along with whatever unfortunate souls had been taken. Ted approached the officers speaking perfect Vietnamese, showing respect, not confrontation. He was taken to the company commander, he asked again respectfully if he could take home the imprisoned soldier.

"The company commander appeared cocky. 'Why should I do that?' he asks Ted. 'Why don't I just kill you and him, and then I'll have two dead Americans?' Ted said nothing. 'Well, I'll make a deal with you,' the commander continued. 'I'd like to give my troops a little entertainment. I'd like you to provide it for us. Do you see that two-story building out there?'

"'Yes, I passed it on the way in,' Ted answered.

"'Good,' the commander answered. 'You jump from the roof of that building, do a back flip, into a fifty-gallon drum. The drum will be surrounded by landmines. Are you agreeable?'

"Of course Ted had no choice, but I'm pretty sure he would have said yes either way. They set the thing up like a kind of show, you know, with all them ten thousand troops trying to see. And of course, you have to know, old Ted just completely nails the thing to the sheer amazement of that crowd. They thought they'd witnessed a miracle. Well, I guess it was, of sorts.

"Anyway, they took him back to the company commander, who had the soldier in question at hand. The commander approached and whispered into Ted's ear in perfect English, 'I knew you could do it, Buzz!' Ted took the soldier and disappeared into the jungle. It turns out company commander Kwang Bae Nam had been a foreign exchange student at Georgia Tech, but had been expelled from the United States when the Vietnam War began."

The three men just sat there shaking their heads.

Finally, Dave said softly, "That's beautiful. Yeah. That's our guy, Buzz."

Chapter Nine
Black Friday

The remainder of the week proved to be just as damp and chilling as the day of the funeral.

"Beer, Dave?" the bartender asked the older man.

"Sure, thanks," Schwelfer answered.

The thoughtful bartender, out of consideration for Dave's privacy, had set a martini glass in front of the barstool next to him. Dave noted it gratefully. He loved his buddies, but while he needed to be with them, he wanted to spend the time just thinking and remembering, not talking. Occasionally Sue would walk up behind him, pat him on the back and ask, "Y'all right?"

"Yes, yes," he'd say nodding. But in his mind, he was remembering daily jogs around Atlanta with Buzz. Hearing more about his dear, lost friend had done little to ease the sting of the loss. He'd known Buzz to be a strong, respectable man, with a great deal of healthy mischief in him. But he'd never known the extent of his valor—or brain power for that matter.

"Flick on that CNN," somebody said down the bar from him.

TV was good, Dave thought. It's a way of mellowing the pain. Maybe I'll tune in for a while.

"'Nother, Dave?" the bartender said.

"Sure," Dave answered. It was 3:30, just the time Buzz would be leaving work, he thought. He cast his eyes upward to the television screen. At first, it was a blur, but eventually, he caught on to the news. Then, it hit.

"Atlanta's Mayor William Campbell announced a change this afternoon in the city's housing structure," the announcer read. "Roosevelt Towers, a high rise senior citizens' home located at the corner of North Avenue and Techwood Drive in Atlanta has been released for sale. The mayor stated that the asking price for the older building located in central Atlanta is set at fifteen million dollars, and most likely resigned to accommodate businesses. Currently Roosevelt Towers houses five hundred and fifty elderly residents, mostly at rents regulated by the state. The mayor has assured them that they will be relocated to other homes around the city. No relocation will take place, however, until after the Olympics this summer…"

The announcer continued, but Dave felt the hand on his beer go numb. He turned away from the screen.

"Just what he needs to hear…" he heard Sue saying somewhere behind him.

He finished his beer quickly, and walked the few hundred yards to his home at Roosevelt Towers. Inside, he found his friends, neighbors, and even some members of the media in an uproar.

"Did you hear what they said on the television?" a white-haired lady in a wheelchair demanded. "Did you hear that report?"

"I did, yeah," he nodded, anxious to get away.

"Well, it's not right," she said. "It isn't right to the citizens."

"No, it isn't," he said. Dave wondered fleetingly about the disastrous affect such an occurrence would have on the listening team next door to Boner's apartment. Just as he reached the elevator, a paramedics team burst through the entry to the building.

"Excuse us, please, emergency," the lead man repeated as they parted the group in the lobby. "Emergency, please move to the sides. Thank you."

They entered the elevator and the doors closed behind them. Dave turned around to see if he recognized anyone in the hall.

The old-lady was at his elbow. "Old Mr. Ridmore," she said. "He was ninety. As soon as he heard, his nurse said, he just laid down and died from the shock. His heart couldn't take it."

Dave sat down. There was no hurry to get upstairs, he decided. Soon enough he'd see Jack, Bob, and Marvin. They'd all have to talk. The relocation was inconceivable. Maybe Ridmore bought it, but he didn't. All of these folks have lives, here, he reasoned. Not many of us still drive. We all get around on foot, or the shuttles. How can they justify taking apart so many lives? They don't even relocate school children anymore. And how much less helpless are some of these residents than children?

"Hiya, Dave," Marvin said, slumping onto the bench beside him. "I guess you heard."

"I sure did," Dave said. "But I can't believe it."

"You don't think they'll sell?"

"How can they do that?"

"What, sell it right from under us?" Jack said, joining them. "Where's Arnold?"

"Maybe we should ask his neighbor," Marvin scoffed.

"Seriously, you think they'll sell?" Dave repeated.

"Sure they will, Schwelfer," Marvin answered. "They got no reason not to."

"But some of these residents are, you know, housebound. And others get out and around on foot. How are these people supposed to continue with their lives in some new location miles from here? How are we?"

"I didn't say it was a good idea," Marvin said. "I just think if they can make a buck or two, they're gonna do it."

"No question about that," said Jack.

Bob came through the doors carrying two bags of groceries. "What's all this about?"

"You haven't heard?" Marvin asked incredulously.

"I been on watch," he explained. "Hi Dave, Jack."

"Yeah, well, it appears that we are about to lose our residence. It's up for sale for development—office building, you can be sure."

Bob shook his head. "They said it could happen, but I didn't believe it."

"Well, I still don't," said Dave. "There's got to be something we can do about it. How about all the volunteers for Tech that live here—and the students? How about the Roosevelt Investment Club?" he asked, his voice softening. He referred to one of many well-organized groups comprised of sep- and octogenarians. This one met daily in the lobby to exchange ideas and share the *Wall Street Journal.* Fridays, they'd dress up in coat and tie and head down to the Merrill Lynch Office three blocks away to catch the big tape, and partake of the activities of the savvy investment firm. In the preceding year, the group had gained nineteen percent on their investments. They'd been encouraged by the success, and determined to keep the upward trend in motion. What would they do, Dave wondered. "How will those fellows meet every day if they're miles apart? How are they gonna make it down to Merrill Lynch together if it's thirty miles instead of three blocks?"

"Yeah," Bob said, nodding. "And then there's old Leonard marching man Tate. I don't think they have too many parades out Athens way. What if he's so far out of the city he can't join in another parade?"

"That old guy's been marching since the sixties," Marvin said. "I know he said he was in the protest march the day King was shot."

"That's what I heard, too," Jack said. "And what about everything else? You got the whole *Towers Monthly Newsletter.*

It's a freakin' institution! How can all this just get ripped apart because somebody doesn't like rent controls?" His voice cracked. "You know," he continued bravely, his voice clearly wavering, "I think I could stomach losing another one of us more easily than seeing the whole thing split up like this."

"Amen to that," Marvin said. "It's criminal, it really is."

"You should know, Marvin," Bob said, trying to lighten things. "And you're right."

"Look," Dave insisted, "I just don't see how it's possible. OK. I don't mean that. I mean I don't see how it's *im*-possible for us to do something—something! We know people—Marvin, you got friends…"

"It take a whole lotta friends to stop this snowball rolling, Dave," Marvin answered sadly.

"Well, maybe…maybe I'll hit the PowerBall, maybe I'll raise the fifteen million," he said.

"I think we got more chance of that than of convincing these clowns not to sell," Jack said.

"Well, I'll give it my best shot," Dave said, a bittersweet smile on his face.

Chapter Ten
The Idea

Dave Schwelfer headed for the Yellow Jacket Bar a little after 7:00 later that week. It was a late April evening, and as he headed west up over the hill, he caught sight of the Coca Cola tower high in the sky. On that night, a magnificent sunset glowed in the sky, seeming to surround the tower with a dazzling effervescence. Dave didn't know if it was due to the extraordinary emotion he'd undergone in such a short time, but he knew that something special was happening. For a moment, he was sure he saw Buzz in his Georgia Tech yellow jacket mascot suit, his number twenty-five clearly printed across it. And he heard Buzz's voice repeating, "This is the way, this is the way."

Dave was overwhelmed, certain he'd received an answer to his torment; an answer from God. It was then that the idea struck him. And by the time he entered the bar, it had grown so much in his mind that he needed to go home and work things out on paper.

"Here you go, Dave," said the bartender, a beer in hand.

"No thanks," Dave said. "I'll just have a glass of water tonight."

"Water? Are you feeling all right?"

"Yeah, yeah. I'm good. In fact, I'll tell you what. I can't stick around. Would you do me a favor and tell the guys I'll be at the prayer meeting tomorrow night at Jack's?"

"No problem, Dave. Take it easy."

The next night, the sign was up on Jack McBride's apartment door, and all were present, but the atmosphere was heavy with missing Buzz. Harry, the president and de facto leader, opened the meeting in much the same way as usual, but, sensing Dave's urgency and having spoken with him earlier, he simply said, "Mr. Schwelfer—Dave—would like to address us, now."

Ordinarily, everybody present would have had some kind of wise crack or fast remark to make, but on that evening, it was very quiet. The members of the group saw the intensity on Dave's face and remained attentive and encouraging.

"Listen," Dave began, "I know half you guys—or all you guys—are going to think I've finally gone over the edge. But I need to share a couple of things with you, as they say, and the first one is the kicker."

He paused to see where his "audience" was, how they were taking him.

"Go on, Dave," Bob said. "We're listening."

He swallowed and cleared his throat. "OK. Well, here's how it happened. You see, last night I was just getting back to the Yellow Jacket. I'd been there, then gone to Elsie's birthday party, and on the way, it was sunset, you know. I looked up as I headed up that hill, and it was an incredible sight. It wasn't just your typical spring sunset. It was more like one of those celestial kinds you see in the movies—you know, like Song of Bernadette?"

Jack and Marvin nodded.

"Well, I happened to notice that the glow, this incredible gathering of light and color was all centered on—of all things—the Coca Cola Tower. As I walked along, I could swear I saw Buzz out there—no, no, guys, I'm not loosing it. I mean it. I saw him in his mascot outfit just for a moment, and I heard his voice. He was saying, 'This is the way, this is the way.'

"I got the overwhelming feeling that he was sending me a message about this Roosevelt Towers situation. He had a way that we could save the building and all of the residents from upheaval." Dave paused for a sip of water.

Marvin and Harry exchanged glances.

"Really, I'm OK," he said.

"No, go on, go on," said Marvin. "You know *I* wanna hear it!"

"It didn't take long for me to start forming the idea," Dave continued. "Even by the time I'd reached the bar, I had a beginning. That's why I left, you know. I had to get my thoughts down and see, just see if it made any sense whatsoever.

"Well, here it goes. I found out today that the Coca Cola Bottling Company keeps one of the world's best kept secrets—the formula for Coca Cola—right there, in that tower, on the twenty-fifth floor."

Dave paused.

"Well...what are you saying?" Bob asked, tentatively.

"I guess, well, you know, I guess I'm saying that if we happened to get our hands on that formula, we could sell it for what it might cost us to somehow reappropriate the Towers, here."

The room was so quiet, you could have heard a rabbit fart. But the tension was one of excitement; of wheels turning and wood burning.

"Wait," Harry said, officiously holding up a hand. "Before we go any further with this idea, we need to know who's in and who's out. No pressure. But we need an honest assessment of what the group thinks."

"Why don't we just vote on it?" Marvin said. "A secret ballot would be best."

And so it was that Dave's idea was approved—eight in favor, zero opposed.

"All right!" Harry announced, "The Ays have it. I think we need to think through what each of us can do to work out a reasonable plan."

"Reasonable?" Mike laughed.

"I agree, but you know what I mean," Harry said. "Mike, you're so excellent in research. You think you could find out some interesting things for us?"

"I've never tried to scope out Coke," Mike said. "It would be a pleasure—and a challenge, I think."

"What would you look for?" Gary asked.

"Ways in, formula location, building information, anything, really," Mike answered.

"Good," Harry answered. "Tex, you and Gary are the engineering team. Maybe you can work out details for electrical and structural clearance and entry. What might be done to clear the way, and ways we could manage the mission."

"You got it," Tex said.

"Yeah," Gary said. "We'll get to work on it tomorrow—tonight later, maybe."

"I think I'll be able to find out a little about the security arrangements," Marvin offered. "There's still plenty of guys in there I know."

"All right, that's a great start," Harry said.

The next week arrived in rapid order.

"How about an opening prayer, Marvin?" Harry asked.

Marvin heard the sincerity in his voice. "OK," he said. And that time, there was no room for jokes. Marvin spoke as a coach would before an important game. His genuineness and depth was felt by all.

When he'd finished, he sat down and took out some notes he'd made. "I think I'll destroy these as soon as I report," he said, smiling.

"Good idea," said Bob.

"OK. Briefly, there's a ten-foot iron fence that totally surrounds the Coca Cola compound. They got ten, maybe twelve guards on duty during the week from 5:00 am to 9:00 pm. Then they cut back to five guards on the weekends, from 9:00 pm to 5:00 am. On top of that, they got three guards on seven nights a week; two stationed at the main lobby, covering a console of about thirty security cameras that service the entire area, inside and out. The third one is stated on the twenty-fifth floor—you got it! In front of the vault. But he's got to watch a five-screen console that are set up only in the upper five levels of the building, the executive floors."

"Great work, Marvin!" Dave said joyously.

"No, wait. There's more," he said smiling. "Right around 10:00 pm every night of the week, the cleaning crew arrives. They start on the twentieth floor, and work their way down. Once they're done, one of the guards from the lobby goes up to the twentieth floor, switches off the lights on each floor, and secures it before he moves down to the next floor. The guard takes about forty to fifty minutes to manage this task. The guard watching the five-level console does the same for the upper levels."

"Great stuff," Harry said. "Nice work, Marvin. Any questions?"

"Yeah," Mike said. "Are the guards employees of Coke, or from some outside service?"

"You know, I didn't find that out," Marvin answered. "But I can. I'll try to get a hold of answer for you by next week."

"OK, and could you find out what the make and model is on the security cameras they use?" Mike asked.

"Absolutely," Marvin said, nodding.

"How about you, Tex?" Harry asked. "You find out something for us?"

"Yes. It seems that the vault is protected by a laser beam system. Additionally, it has its own back-up generator in case of power failure." He made a face. "So it's pretty impossible to turn the beams off. But I think I have an idea involving refracting the light as a way to get around this problem. Give me a week to work it out, and I'll let you know how we can handle it."

"I took a pretty thorough tour of the compound," Gary said. "As far as weak spots or possible entry points, there aren't too many. I'd like to work with you on one way they could get in. But I've got an idea for an exit point, but it would involve a little doing. We'd create a big banner, heavy canvas, saying something along the lines of Welcome to the Olympics, or whatever. But disguised within its support cables, we could have an exit to the outside via pulley and cable."

Harry's eyes lit up.

"And one thing that might help in planning entry is to decide when we're going to attempt this thing," Gary continued.

"During the Olympics," Jack said. "I think during the Olympics would be an ideal time. The attention to the building and its various security requirements would be low, and on top of that, there are likely to be a lot of extra people coming and going from the building. We'd have a better shot then than at a time when there are only regulars milling around, who all know each other."

"That sounds like a good premise to go on," Harry said. "What does everybody else think?"

After it had been agreed that the Olympics would be the target date, Harry doled out a few more assignments. "I'm hatching a master plan," he said. "But we'll need to get as much information on this thing as we can."

They played a few hands of cards, but the game was decidedly not the same as with Buzz, and no one wanted to fake enthusiasm.

"It sure isn't the same without our mascot, huh, guys?" Dave said.

"Never will be," Bob agreed.

Five days later, the enthusiasm level was accelerated. It was a big adventure, way surpassing the airport caper and any others that they had attempted in the past. Dave thought of Buzz and his many missions he had accomplished completely alone in the hell land of Vietnam. "One little thing," he said to himself, "if we can do just this one little thing now, I think we will have truly gained something by being his friend."

Marvin reported that the guards were hired by Brink's, an outside guard service, and that Rollins was both the maker and servicing contractor for the security cameras.

"Wait till you hear this next report," Harry said, smiling.

"It turns out," Mike said, "that I was able to get the combination for those steel doors of the vault."

Everyone applauded, spontaneously.

"With Marvin's new info, I should be able to get something on the internal safe and the security cameras, too, by next week," he said grinning proudly.

"You're such a geek," Gary said.

"Yeah," Mike agreed. "Don't cha love it?"

Chapter Eleven
Harry Needs to be Alone

With the wheels turning so quickly, Harry, as the leader of the group, felt a strong need to get some quiet time. There was certainly a lot of able manpower, and almost an army of brainpower to go with it. Thoughts of Mike's eventual success in the business world almost gave him a chill. The guy was brilliant. But what, he wondered, would happen if he, the planner, made any mistakes?

No. That was the answer. He simply could not make mistakes. And in order to assure himself that the operation would work, he headed out to his very own special spot. Harry had always attracted trust, and, even as a freshman, he had been a ticket collector at the stadium ball games. Somehow, he had ended up with a key to Bobby Dodd Stadium, long after his duties in the ticket department were over. He was discreet, and never excessive with the privilege, but Harry did enjoy the occasional romantic interlude, overlooking the magnificent Atlanta skyline from high atop the stadium in the upper southwest corner. Such had become his spot.

On that day in May, as the start of the Olympic Games approached, Harry dropped into a seat and took a deep breath. "Start big, and work to the fine points," he mumbled. "Get the big picture, and shimmy it down to the details."

And there he sat, pencil and pad in hand, scribbling, drawing, erasing, thinking, and angsting for the entire afternoon and into the evening. Around dinner time, he started to smile. He'd worn his pencil down so far it was just about impossible to make it write anymore, but he knew what he wanted. And he knew how he wanted it done. But he wasn't sure how to approach. After a time, he rose, his plan in his head and somewhat on paper, with one important raw material yet to secure—the *ettes.*

"No, I mean, you have to promise," he said.

Maggie shook her head. "I *promise.* I *promise promise promise!* How many times do I have to say it? Who would I tell anyway?"

"That's not important. You have to swear to secrecy, even if I tell you. Then, after that, you have to double swear if you decide…"

"If I decide what, Harry? This is weird. Are you sure you're all right?"

Harry smiled. "I'm great," he said. "I feel terrific. And I know I can trust you. I'm sorry. I'm just letting my emotional fine tuning get the best of me."

The waitress stopped by to take their drink order. Then Harry picked up again.

"Thanks for coming out tonight, too, by the way. I know you're studying hard."

"You know I'll always have time for you," she said. "Tell me what's up."

"Ah, music to my ears!" he said, taking her hand for a moment, and bringing it to his lips.

Maggie smiled. "Come on!"

Harry laughed. "OK, but move forward so I don't have to broadcast this to every Tom, Dick and Hattie in the place.

Some time later, Maggie sat fascinated, her eyes and heart aglow.

"You know, your reaction surprises me somewhat."

"Really?"

"Not just that you get it, and that you fully understand it, because this isn't really your thing, but also that you're so fearlessly ready to go with it."

"I think it's the right thing to do," she answered. "I know that technically it's wrong, but there's a fine line here for me. Is the goal correct? Yes. Is the method dangerous to anyone? Not really. Does it sound like a total blast? Yes."

Harry laughed. "You would be integral, you know. Seriously important. You'd be one of the three break-in artists." He mouthed the last three words to keep from saying it out loud.

"I know," Maggie mouthed back. "And I'm absolutely thrilled!" She leaned forward to give him a kiss. "I can't tell you what it means to me that you have that kind of confidence in me. Really. It means an awful lot, Harry."

Harry sighed. "And I have good planning power."

"You're a top notch schemer," she agreed, giggling.

"Here's the thing. What are the chances that the rest of the *ettes* will feel the same?"

"You know what? You just have to ask them. That's all. We'll all get together and discuss it."

"Right. We'll meet Sunday for lunch at my spot. But man, let's eat now. I'm starved!"

That Sunday afternoon, the *ettes* dutifully traipsed behind Harry and Maggie up the long journey to Harry's spot. Marta and Charlotte, both in excellent shape, executed the climb without a struggle. Fitz, on the other hand, was another story.

"This better be worth it!" she puffed, taking a breath between every other word. As she reached the top and took a seat, she looked Harry squarely in the eye. "So, ever get laid up here?"

The group burst into fits of laughter.

"No," Harry answered indignantly. "What kind of person do you think I am?"

Maggie, however, subtly averted her eyes, but blushed nevertheless.

Fitz appeared not to notice. "You know, when I was your age, fifty years ago, I too, had a favorite spot. My grandparents had a ninety-acre farm in the red hills. Aside from grazing a herd of milkers, and thirty-five riding horses, they grew fields and fields of wheat. It was a pleasure to behold, even for a kid. Well they had a thirty-five-foot high barn, with a double loft and legume hay for the taking. It was spectacular. Right in the midst of those bales, with that incredible freshness and aroma, was my special spot." She paused to give Harry another look. "No, don't even bother asking. I christened the place during my freshman year at college!"

Everybody laughed.

It was a casual meeting, with Charlotte and Fitz discussing those old days just as easily as they discussed the plan with the younger folks. Harry explained that it was OK if they chose not to participate. There was no pressure. But, on the other hand, everyone was welcome, and most certainly could and would be useful if they decided to join in.

"What the guys did," Harry said, "was to write a secret ballot—yes, or no. Maggie has already agreed. She's going to be in the thick of it with Gary and Tex to do the actual pilferage. Your roles would be less direct, as I explained, but just as important."

"I vote we take a vote," Fitz said. "And just so the guys have nothing on us, I think it ought to be secret, too."

And so it was that the *ettes* were not to be outdone by their male counterparts. The vote was quickly three in favor, zero opposed. All were in!

The sign one passed during that time under the Marta Station flashed electronic updates on the countdown of days before the Olympics were to begin. As the members of the elite groups of *F.A.R.T.S.*and *ettes* passed through, the message was received far less casually.

The right timing was essential, according to Harry's plan. It was a thorough rendering, there was no question of that. As such, one of the first actions to be put in motion early that month of May was a sort of psychological preparation of sorts. Harry requested that Mike create a relatively regular security monitor interference for periods of about thirty seconds three to four times a week at around the same time of day each time. The first several episodes of Mike's successful snowing of the screens sent urgent calls to the repair and maintenance crew from Coca Cola headquarters. On each occasion, however—and since there was nothing actually wrong with the monitors—the repairmen reported that the system was working fine and that there was not problem. On about the third or fourth visit, one serviceman suggested that perhaps the interference was being caused by the increased activity in the area, with the Olympics and all. The idea settled well with the internal security personnel, who eventually accustomed themselves to the snowy screen for periods of thirty seconds or so every so often.

"Fellow told me that it's because of the Olympic computers coming in," Marvin told Harry with a chuckle. "He says he's not worried about it. As long as it keeps on working, and there's no mess-up with the recording devices. I guess we'd better make sure they take a powder, too, during the process."

"Thanks, you're right," Harry said. "I have that pretty much covered, but I'll double check it all with Tex, the electrical man."

The time was slipping away, and there was still a lot to be done before D-Day. "You've got a handle on getting the building plans, right Gary?" Harry asked.

"Yeah, and Mike's gonna help me do it so the terminal we send it to isn't traceable to us in any way."

"Good. And Marta, you and Charlotte are getting things set for the Trojan Horse, and Olympic flag, right?"

Marta nodded. "It's going good, Harry."

"Great. And I want you, Tex and Mike to relax about work."

"You got something?"

"I didn't do it. Mike, the wizard, set everybody up as floor hosts for their dorm. You guys are still residents even after you graduate!"

"That's better than you know," Gary said. "We're only two doors down from Roosevelt Towers—but we're also rooftop privileged—we can see Coca Cola easy, at any time."

"And that's what we want. Charlotte's gonna work her magic this afternoon," Harry said. "Are you ready, Charlotte?"

"Yes, I think so," she said. "We've got the credit card billing set up, right? I don't want the call to show up identified on caller ID."

"Yes, it's here. Just dial this number first, then City Hall."

Charlotte was solid as a rock. "Hello, yes, City Clerk? Hi, this is Emily Sarnstandt with the Atlanta Committee for the Olympics. May I have building permits, please?"

Harry and Maggie exchanged glances. The woman was a pro.

"Hi, yes. Thank you. Listen, I'm sending over two gentleman this afternoon if it's convenient. They need to review the plans of some of the buildings located on North Avenue. There will be several foreign dignitaries visiting, you see, and we have a pretty hefty security obligation…yes, that's right. Well, again, I'm Emily Sarnstandt, uh huh, and the gentlemen's names are Mr. Lemons and Mr. McBride."

After she hung up, the group celebrated, high-fiving their senior impersonator, and toasting her outstanding cool.

"Did you just work that up for us—for this thing?" Tex asked.

"Oh, no, dear," she said. "It takes years."

Everyone laughed. And sure enough, that afternoon, the Atlanta city officials in the Building Department went out of their way to accommodate their two older, distinguished colleagues. Lemons and McBride came away with the booty--copies of the building plans for the Coca Cola Tower.

Meanwhile, Tex and the *ettes* put hours in every day on creating the bottle-shaped Trojan Horse. It was to be a spectacular work, requiring almost two thousand prisms to complete. It would stand six feet tall. The work went on in secret at the basement of the group's dormitory.

Gary and Mike managed to create the impression, via a system of elaborate faxes and emails, that one of the advertising executives or assistants within Coca Cola had come up with the idea for the giant Olympic Flag to be hung across North Avenue. Gary constructed the cable system to support the enormous décor. The task was complete and on display by Memorial Day weekend.

Some of the participants would be arriving in early June from foreign countries, although the Olympics were to take place in July. Marvin determined it was necessary to begin a training program in June so as to get his three robbers in shape. They would need to be perfectly fit for their assignment.

Chapter Twelve
The Vault

Later that month, Marvin reviewed with the three and Harry the details of the vault that their mission was to penetrate. "It's not really a vault in the typical sense. I mean, when you see it, you'll know what I mean. But for now, try to picture the average-sized home. Twenty-four hundred square feet. That's how big this thing is."

"Twenty-four hundred square feet!" Tex said. "That's a shocker."

"Yeah, and it's not just a few shelves and things. It's got displays like, try to picture it," Marvin continued. "Inside are treasures, like Van Goghs, and Monets, Picassos, all kinda gold and silver jewelry. Collectible from the Middle Ages and beyond. Incredible stuff. They are up, most of them displayed. There are photographs. If you had the time, which you won't, you'd see photos of all kinds of folks drinking Coke, all the United States Presidents from FDR forward, Popes John the Twenty-Third, Paul the Sixth, and John Paul the Second, Gandhi, Martin Luther King as a child, even Hitler and Mussolini."

"No shit!" said Harry. "How'd you find that out?"

"I was just talking to one of the guys," Marvin answered. "You know, of course I felt like an absolute bandit, but hey, they love to talk. They don't mind sharing with an old APD guy."

"I'm all for sharing," Maggie said.

"Listen, this vault is so valuable, they honestly have a curator for it, just the vault."

Everybody sighed.

"Woah," breathed Harry.

"The only people allowed inside the vault are the president of Coke, the four executive VPs, two chairmen of the board of directors, and of course, the curator. If anyone was so highly privileged to be shown the inside of that vault, it was mandatory—steel arm mandatory—that one of the people allowed in accompanied the privileged guest."

"The thing is, the formula you need isn't in the vault outright. It sits inside a separate safe that actually inside the first vault. If that's not enough, the safe it sits inside is actually an antique itself. It was apparently the original safe kept in Asa Candler's office, back in 1910. And the only thing inside *that* safe," Marvin paused for dramatics, "is the high coveted, much sought after, and extensively imitated, almost priceless formula for the most celebrated and recognized beverage in the world!

"The only, the *only* guy who's allowed to look inside that safe is the president of the company, Kenneth Carlson. And the last time that happened was twelve years ago when they moved into the complex.

"Well, it sounds as if we have to make it into two securities then, after the office itself," said Gary.

"See, you have to understand. Like we discussed before, there's only about a forty-minute time period when that guard is away from this thing. Forty minutes in the entire day, which comes right after the cleaning crew is done doing their thing and the guard goes and secures each of the top five floors. Aside from penetrating the office, you've got to get through the heavy, Oak, wooden door first. Once that is open, you reach the steel door with our combination lock, and then you get into the separate safe with the actual formula inside.

"As you know there are security cameras inside and outside that vault. They are monitored at the front and main security stations in the lobby. On top of that, there are laser beams everywhere. If the particle flow of any beam is disturbed while you are in that vault, the steel door, which is very very thick, will close rapidly and instantly. You can't get out. You're locked inside to enjoy the music. And the music plays by way of alarms to the front and main console, the upper floor level console, and both Brinks and Rollins headquarters.

"I guess what I'm trying to say is, don't disturb the particle flow."

Gary, Tex, and Maggie sat dead silent, and deep in concentration.

Chapter Thirteen
Paying for the Robbery

Harry had never expected the heist to be cheap, and when all was totaled on his planning pad, he was not surprised to see a total expense in the twenty-thousand-dollar range. Yet, he had few ideas on how to raise the money. The communication system they would need would be the most expensive single item, followed by the two thousand crystals necessary to build their Trojan Coke Bottle, and various other things. He had been delighted with the news Mike had given him earlier that day—he'd cracked the combination on the smaller safe; it had been an easier job than the outside vault. Brains were premium with these guys, he thought, but we sure don't have much money. The students, he knew, had no money of their own, and from what he figured, the seniors had only enough to keep them going. Twenty thousand dollars was an enormous sum, but he had a plan. He had planned on working on the money right along with everything else, from the start.

Harry's plan: Dwight "Napkins" Horton. Napkins was a professional student. He had begun his college education in the late 1970s and by 1996 was working on his second degree, a few courses at a time. But he was a likeable guy, and more recognizable by the student body than the school's president—who had changed more often than Napkins had changed majors. For his trouble, Napkins had secured himself four seats on the fifty-yard line at Bobby Dodd Stadium and center court locations for Bobby

Crimmins basketball games. And over his many years, he had developed his own on-campus conglomerate of services, from carpeting dorm rooms, creating tee-shirts for fraternities and sororities, arranging bus trips, arranging dates, booking bands, booking spring break travel, *and* help with fund raising, always writing the customer's requests for assistance on a napkin. It was this last talent that had led Harry to invite the man out for a beer.

"I like this place," Napkins said, nodding. "Yellow Jacket's a nice spot."

"Yeah, it's great," said Harry.

"So, listen, Bob Arnold said you wanted to talk to me. What's up?"

"Yeah, Napkins. I've got a money issue, and I thought you might be the one to come up with some good ideas."

"How much we talkin' 'bout?"

"Twenty thousand, give or take a few thousand."

"Well, hell, Harry, you ain't gonna get that selling tee-shirts!"

Harry laughed. "They'd probably have to be designers."

"What on earth you need so much cash for?"

"We'd like to buy a van. We've got a club. Half of its members live at the Roosevelt Towers down the street there. Their building is being sold come fall and the residents are all getting relocated. With a van, we figure we can transport folks back and forth. It could be used by other residents or by those who work or have activities on campus."

"Hmm," said Napkins. "Let me think on it. By the way, I do my best thinking when I have a few beers."

"Hell," Harry laughed, "you can drink all night as long as the ideas keep flowing. I'll even throw in a steak dinner for a great one!"

"Sounds good to me," Napkins said. "I'll tell you, it's a shame your club isn't connected with the University."

"Oh, no, we are!" Harry said. "We're listed as an official organization in the directory of Georgia Tech as the Farternity Among Retirees and Tech Students."

"Well, then that's great. I got two ideas that I think just might work. I have a friend who handles the mailings in the alumni office. Those things go out maybe once a month. My guess is we could get a flier on this included with their next mailing, you know, asking for donations. I'm guessing a lot of the old grads would cough up, and I don't think twenty thousand is out of the question. And secondly, you get this thing going and set up a display for the alumni weekend. You do it right, you could get the figure you're looking for!"

Harry smiled. "So, how do you like your steak?"

It was only a couple of nights later that Dave approached Harry.

"Let me take you to dinner, Harry," Dave said. "I got something I'd like to discuss with you."

"I'll always take time out for dinner," Harry said.

At Trovato's, a wonderful Italian restaurant that Dave and Buzz had frequented, they found themselves welcomed by the bartender, who had heard of Buzz's passing. After Dave and Harry had had a few beers, they headed for a table. There, they were greeted by a couple of Buzz's in and out martinis, compliments of his old buddy behind the bar. The three sipped and toasted Buzz.

"This is a good spot," Harry said.

"Yeah, it's got nice folks and good food," Dave answered.

Well into dinner, Dave handed Harry an envelope. "Open it," he said.

"I'll try anything once," Harry chuckled. Inside, he found a check for twenty-six thousand, two hundred and eighty-seven dollars. It had been made out to Dave Schwelfer. The sight of it was extremely sobering.

"What is this?" Harry asked.

"This is our heist fund," Dave answered flatly.

"No, Dave," Harry answered instinctively. "We can't use this. It's what, your nest egg? Your stocks money?"

"No, it's from Buzz," Dave said. "It's the net proceeds from an amount he left to me. I think he meant it for all of us, Harry."

"But Dave, it's yours!"

"I haven't told a soul about the money," Dave said. "And I haven't gotten attached to it. We're comfortable enough. If we don't need it all, that's fine. But I'd like to be able to anonymously contribute it in some way. I need you to promise that."

"You don't even want anyone to know? How about your wife, Marcia?"

"She doesn't know about it. I have her on a need-to-know-only basis. Honestly, I'd just be more comfortable," Dave said.

Harry nodded. "All right Dave." He smiled. "This is truly amazing."

"You know, when I first saw that sunset and swear to god, heard Buzz's voice, from that point on, it's been like one little miracle after another. You think we can pull this thing off, Harry?"

"I think we can. I really do."

"I sure hope so," said Dave.

Harry looked down. "I'll cash this check and put the money in a safety deposit box with both of our names on it," he said. "Good enough."

"That's fine," Dave said. "Now let's say no more about it."

"How about a couple more of those martinis?" Harry called.

The bartender laughed. "OK, guys, but I'll be driving the both of you home afterwards."

"Done," said Dave.

And he did.

Chapter Fourteen
River Party

The group from the Yellow Jacket bar found themselves at the center of a crossroads. Time was nearing graduation, and the students would be finished with that life and ready to move ahead on their individual paths. But at the same time, they were in the midst of a smaller unfolding drama, and one in which they had devoted heart and soul.

It was decided by the common body that there would be a graduation party in honor of the students, but to be attended by all *F.A.R.T.S.* and *ettes* at a park on the shore of the Chattahoochee River.

The day of the party was warm and sunny.

"Who's up for horse shoes?" Jack called, holding a couple in his hands already.

"I'm waiting to get a team together for volleyball," Marta said. "But I bet Bob'll join in."

"I'm gonna watch—I mean play—volleyball," Bob said.

Maggie laughed. "I'd say watch, depending on who's playing," she said. "A lot of our friends will be here."

"I know," Bob beamed. "And I think it's important to have someone experienced to officiate."

"Well I'm playing shoes," Jack said, walking away. "Let me know if you change your mind."

"Look at this food," said Harry, arriving with Sue and Tim. "I can't believe how much stuff is here already."

"I like to experiment on you guys," Sue said, smiling.

"I think she's just plain generous," Maggie said, sampling a cold shrimp. "Oh, this is good!"

"Let me try that," Marta said. "I'm officially graduated. Time to be sophisticated, grow a little culture."

"And a few extra pounds, string bean," said Maggie, laughing. "When are you going to stop worrying about your weight?"

"Now," Marta said. "Officially, now."

Charlotte arrived with a beautiful centerpiece. She smiled as she set it up on the table. Those nearby smiled in recollection and fondness, but said nothing. The wreath had been made of gloriously scented white carnations.

"Make way, everyone, make way," called Dave. "Keg, comin in."

Dave and Tex were cautiously rolling the large, silver keg toward the gathering, while Mike and Gary crated in the ice.

"They got the hard part," Gary said. "We've got it easy carrying fifty pounds of ice that doesn't roll."

"Ah, come on!" Harry teased. "Piece of cake! Where's your muscles?"

"Let's see you do it!" Gary said.

"I would, but I can't strain my arms. I need them for volleyball later," Harry said.

The beer was set on top of the ice, tapped, and ready to go. Dave felt obliged to take the poison off. "Yeah," he said, drawing on the ice cold beer. "That's what I call living."

"Where's Fitz?" Harry asked, grabbing a cup.

"She's pulling up now," Maggie said. "And that's Marvin right ahead of her, I think."

Fitz had brought a large sign that said "Congratulations Graduates" on one side, and a picture of the group—with Buzz—from their earlier days at the Yellow Jacket Bar. The picture started them reminiscing.

"This has definitely been one of the most refreshing chapters of my life," Fitz said. "I never expected to find myself in a group this alive and full of fun so late in life."

"I have to say the same," said Charlotte, "and it's been more than just fun. It's been really helpful in my life, just going through everyday things and having such a wide perspective to listen to and enjoy once or twice a week."

"Are you two gonna gab all day or play ball?" Jack asked.

"We'll probably do a little of each," Fitz said. "Are you going to whine all day or be a man?"

Everyone burst out laughing, including Jack.

"You know how to hurt a guy," he said.

"I think you asked for that one," Marvin said.

"I do my best when necessary," Fitz said, tipping cups with Jack.

The teams were assembled, and the game began. It was much less a competition than another opportunity to laughter and recollections. Eventually, a tie was declared for lack of interest and Jack parlayed Bob, Marvin, and Harry down to the horse shoe field.

"You're gonna love this," he kept saying.

"I think I last played when I was seven," Harry said. "And I lost."

"Oh, this is fun," Jack went on. "Tell him, you guys."

"It's fun," Bob and Marvin said simultaneously, and completely void of enthusiasm.

"Oh, come on…"

As their voices trailed off, Charlotte looked at Dave. "How are ya doin' there, old timer?" she teased.

"Not so bad," Dave said, "for someone who's over the hill."

"I'm glad we could do this. These kids are spectacular."

"They really are. This has been a terrific couple of years. I guess we knew it had to come to an end sometime, though."

"Well, it's not over yet."

"No, not all of it."

Charlotte could see the reminiscence in Dave's eyes. "You'll probably miss him a long time, but there's so much to laugh about, too," she said.

"I know," he said quietly. "I was just thinking how much he would have loved this."

"Yeah, he would have. He would have been watching, and making all of us laugh, just like usual," Charlotte agreed. A breeze blew through, toppling Fitz's sign. Dave studied the faces. "This is a treasure," he said. "More than anything, no matter what happens, this is a treasure."

Fitz approached to tap herself another beer. "So what's going on in this corner of the world?" she asked.

"We were just talking about how great this thing has been, like you and I did earlier," Charlotte said. "You know, before it gets too late, I'd like to do a ceremonial toss into the river. Just to remember Buzz by."

"You're not going to jump in yourself, are you?" Fitz joked.

"Maybe I should!" she laughed. "That would spice things up!"

The group was gradually recongregated around the food table as Tim and Sue went for a walk and a breath of fresh air. The group gradually recongregated around the food table.

"I wonder," Charlotte began, "if it might not be a bad idea to use that carnation centerpiece as a kind of living tribute to our lost friend."

"I think that would be a very nice gesture," Dave said. "I really do."

Everyone quickly agreed.

"But before we do anything," Fitz said, "I think we should have our ceremonial," she tapped the top of a container on the table with ice around it, "birdbath in and out martini!"

Everyone cheered spontaneously. They began to pour each other hefty paper cups of the mixture, which Theodore Anderson, Jr. had made such a familiar and now cherished ritual.

"OK, I'll make the first toast," Dave said. "To the instigator of our latest caper."

Everyone laughed. "Do you think Buzz would have joined in, him being with Coca Cola and all?" Maggie asked.

"I think so," said Marta. "He was full of energy."

"Yeah, but remember, he didn't do the airport one because he didn't want to be dishonest," Maggie said. "Isn't that why?" she asked Harry.

"I don't know," Harry said thoughtfully. "I can't remember."

"She's right," Dave said. "It's funny, I feel as if he gave us the idea. But you're right, Maggie, I don't think he'd have participated in it himself."

"You think he would have put in his two cents worth?" Fitz asked. "Given up a little information, being on the inside and all?"

"No, probably not openly," Dave said. "But one thing is for sure, he would have thought it was all hysterical!"

One hour later, eight friends of Buzz walked together in a group, Charlotte carrying her beautiful carnation handiwork, to the edge of the Chattahoochee River. In silence, and with a few tears, the wreath was tossed over the edge into the swirling waters, where it gently spun, touching rocks and vegetation along the way, and drifted off out of sight.

Chapter Fifteen
The Accident

Music had always been a way of life for Tex, despite his astute ability in engineering. It was his way of communicating, if not to anyone in particular, from very particular feelings. Mostly those feelings were joy and exultation, or just general rowdiness. As the time approached for the Olympics, and teams arrived, Tex had occasion to hang out on campus with Bob, never one to give up a good spot in the park, and occasionally he would take his horn and play some familiar arrangement.

"You got a nice sound, there," came a clipped voice from behind him.

Tex turned to see a tall, very dark-skinned man just a little older than himself. "Well, thanks," he said.

"Mombasa," the fellow said, offering his hand.

"Tex Jenkins," Tex answered, shaking it.

"I got here just about two hour ago," Mombasa declared with a smile, "but I don't tink I ever heard something like that before. You are good!"

"Where ya from, Mombasa?"

"Zambia," he said smiling, his teeth like pearls in the night.

"Zambia—ooh, that's a hot country, huh?"

"Oh yes, it can be!" Mombasa answered. "You know, I am a musician, too."

Tex studied him. "Well, I'd guess you play, let's see…the conga drums?"

"No," Mombasa smiled. "You are not even close!"

Bob was enjoying the exchange. "Ah, come on, Tex, it's obvious."

Mombasa raised his eyebrows. "You know what I play?"

"Hell, yeah," Bob said. "You play the clarinet."

Mombasa's eyes bulged out of their sockets, and Tex laughed at the show of surprise. "How did you know?"

"Listen, by the way I'm Bob Arnold. This nitwit here doesn't have the sense to introduce me."

"Pleased to meeting you."

"Thanks," Bob went on. "I watch folks—not like a creep or anything like that. I just enjoy observing people. Some of my friends say I should be a writer, and I bet they're right. Because I know what a person does by the way he carries himself. You are a direct person, mild mannered, and cheerful. That's not a drummer, although some of those traits go with drums. You play melody, it's a sweet sound, and it's often happy. I figured you were either English horn or clarinet. But my instincts told me it was clarinet."

Mombasa laughed a low rumbling laugh. "Guess what?" he said. "I play English horn, too!"

The friendship between Tex and his musical compadre grew rapidly. Mombasa was a long distance runner and actually predicted internationally to take the gold in the marathon to be held as the final event at the close of the track and field competition. The two could be heard playing in counterpoint and fugue formations from the top of Burge Dorm on Harry's "Up There."

It was during the first week of games that Tex decided he'd treat his friend Mombasa, as well as Charlotte, who'd long expressed an appreciation for symphony music, to a concert held by the Atlanta Symphony Orchestra. The three made quite a stunning combination; Tex in a stark black and white tuxedo with starched collar and tails, Charlotte in an elegant, flowing white dress, and Mombasa in full dress colors from his native Zambia.

"Is that what they wear around in Zambia all the time?" Tex asked him.

"Oh yes," Mombasa answered, stifling a laugh. "They shop for groceries in Lusaka with these outfits on. It helps to distinguish them from the livestock."

"I think he's having fun with you," Charlotte said.

Mombasa burst into his deep, jovial laughter. "This is about as common in Zambia as what you are wearing now is common in Atlanta, US," he said.

"OK, OK, I get it," said Tex. "Boy, ask a simple question…"

The three enjoyed a splendid concert and strolled back through town along the sidewalk, reenacting some of the selections. All at once, Tex broke into a vociferous rendition of "Singing in the Rain." Charlotte and Mombasa, charmed by his antics, joined in along behind him. Mombasa swirled Charlotte around, imitating nearly every segment of the dance done on screen by Gene Kelly and Debbie Reynolds.

"Thank God we're not doing "Make 'em Laugh!" she called out to Tex as they simulated the umbrella segment.

"Oh, come on, you're a pro!" Tex called back.

Mombasa had a terrific time, feeling gloriously happy to be enjoying such wonderful company in the new and amazing country.

"You're a terrific dancer!" Charlotte said to Mombasa as they brought their dance to a conclusion. "Maybe you should be entered in some of the other competitions as well."

"I don't think they have a dancing one—" Mombasa began.

At just that instant, a child jetted out of the Varsity Restaurant, and, without looking ran straight into the heavy traffic on North Avenue. Both Tex and Mombasa instinctively scrambled to retrieve the boy. Tex got to the little fellow first, scooped him up and literally tossed him to the waiting Mombasa, who pushed him forth onto the sidewalk. In that same instant, Tex was hit by a truck coming from one direction, while Mombasa was struck by a car coming from the other.

Another woman might have let out a blood curdling scream, and buried her face in her hands. But Charlotte, a forty-year veteran nurse, headed straight for the victims, barking out order to the stunned pedestrians nearby. "Call 911. Immediately!" she said. "Let them know there are two victims, both hit by cars, one appears to be unconscious. Do it now!"

Next she checked out Tex who was unmoving on the pavement. "Looks like you've broken your playing wrist, pal," she said softly to his unconscious form. "But you're breathing OK, and your pulse feels good under the circumstances.

"Get that traffic away from here!" she called to a policeman. "Move things away so the ambulance can get here!"

"That was my plan," the policeman muttered. "Don't I know how to do my job?"

Next Charlotte examined Mombasa, who was coming to, but moaning hideously. "Can you hear me? Mombasa—can you hear me?"

"Yes, I think so," he said lightly.

Charlotte determined that his knee or leg, or possibly both, had been injured. "Lie still," she told him. "The ambulance will be here soon. That was a beautiful thing you did."

Mombasa lay back, a gentle smile curving his lips. "You mean the dancing?" he said.

As soon as the medical vehicles arrived, Charlotte grabbed a hold of a student from Tech. "Listen, can you please do us a big favor? Run down to Burge Dorm and get Marvin Lemons, who's on duty tonight. Let him know that

Tex and Mombasa got hurt and that we're heading to Crawford Long Hospital."

"You got it," the young man answered, and hurried off.

Charlotte rode in the ambulance. Although the entire event took less than thirty minutes, by the time the ambulance pulled into the emergency bay, local and national news crew—with camera personnel—were setup and ready to report. Marvin arrived shortly thereafter, with Harry, Marta, and Mike.

By 1:00 am, when Dr. Robert Jarrett from the Emergency Room addressed the press, there were nearly two hundred reporters, with camera crew and satellite feeds hungry for the details to fuel the exciting Olympic Games human interest sensation. As Jarrett spoke, his remarks were translated into seventy-two languages and relayed to over one hundred countries.

"Mombasa," he explained, "was lucky enough to avoid head injuries. But, unfortunately, his left leg is very badly bruised. We will be testing later for knee injury, however, we feel in time, there is no reason why he cannot fully recover."

Before the doctor was able to report on Tex's condition, he was bombarded with questions about Mombasa's competitive likelihood in the Olympics.

"I cannot answer that question," he said firmly. "Time always plays a factor in injuries. At that moment, I am sure that Mr. Mombasa is quite happy to be alive."

"But how soon will you know if he can run in the marathon?" a reporter insisted, followed by echoes from others.

Tex, his friends learned, had sustained a concussion and a broken wrist. His discharge would likely be speedier than that of his companion.

"This is a predicament," Harry said to everyone the following morning at an emergency meeting. "Tex is simply not going to be able to join us. We are going to need a replacement." Harry had planned so fastidiously that the change at the very last minute was a heavy blow. He struggled to maintain his calm. "It can't be me—I have to stay central, and it can't be Mike. We need him too much to do things that only he can do."

Eventually, by process of elimination, the choices were left at Marta or Marvin.

"I'll be happy to do it," Marvin said calmly. "I've been training these guys and I feel like I'm in just as good a shape. But there is one problem."

Everyone was silent as Marvin struggled with a way to admit his weakness.

"I, well, I have this *issue*," he said, "with heights."

Gary's mouth fell open. "You're a cop!" he said.

Marvin chuckled. "And so I must be invincible," he said.

"Well…"

"No, no, I appreciate your healthy estimation of my capabilities," Marvin said. "And it's almost true."

Everyone laughed lightly.

"Actually, during my last year on the force, I was assigned to a jumper, at the Westin Hotel over there Peachtree Plaza. Some guy had decided it was time to toss in the towel, and I was supposed to rescue the sorry soul. I was wearing a lifeline, like always, but it wasn't taut enough. You can imagine my shock and amazement when we went over the side of that building and fell a full two stories before it caught us up. The jerk on the line of both of our weight almost caused me to lose the guy—and believe me, by then, he had reconsidered his decision to jump. There's nothing like stark reality to suggest a change in plans. Anyway, it took them ten minutes to get us lowered onto the ladder, and had it been another minute, I would have dropped that poor sucker. Something about being a hundred-some feet up in the air, positioned for free fall soured me on the idea of hanging around the outsides of tall buildings."

"I'm OK *inside*," he continued. "It's just outside where I panic."

"Do you think, I mean, with the plan in mind, you'll be able to fill in for Tex? That's asking a lot under the circumstances," Harry said.

"I'll work with you. I think I can find another way to go out. Besides, I'm certain that without proper training, a person will not pull it off. I'm really the only other one qualified. We'll get the job done, don't worry."

Harry remembered the same assurance from Marvin just before they had attempted the airport caper. He felt rock solid inside. "Thanks, Harry."

It was that very afternoon during which the truck would be rented on which the Coca Cola Trojan Bottle would be driven to One Coca Cola Plaza.

Chapter Sixteen
The Robbery

They were through! The security post had passed them through!

"You wanna head over to shipping and receiving," the man at the gate told them. "It's at the back, lower level B."

The big rented truck, carrying Harry, Marta, and the operational ingredients, slowly backed up to the loading dock. The large soft drink icon was moved onto an enormous freight elevator. Less than two minutes later, the security monitors at all locations inside Coca Cola went to snow.

Thirty seconds later, three agile, well-conditioned, pack-laden emissaries had risen from the behind crystal icon, pushed up the hung ceiling in the elevator, and risen to their appointed riding level. When the security monitors began to function properly again, all that was visible on the freight elevator was a small loading team accompanying a big bottle.

When the elevator paused at floor twenty-five, Harry hit the stop button, ostensibly to remove the Coke Bottle. However, doing so allowed the three inside the shaft to climb up via the inside ladder and disappear into their predetermined hiding places. There they would be required to stay stock still, for hours.

As Marta and Harry moved the bottle onto its proper resting place, a small group of Zambian athletes assisted and served to help put post-travel finishing touches on the grand display. Once the bottle was prepared, the ceremony began.

Zambian athletes and officials were on hand to present the token to the Coca Cola Bottling Company

President as a thank you for the efforts made by Coca Cola on behalf of the Zambian Government, affording the team the opportunity to make the trip to the Olympics in Atlanta. It was a brief ceremony, not well documented. But those few members of the press who did attend showed greater concern for the fallen Mombasa, who was still lying in Crawford Long Hospital, than for the presentation at hand. President Kenneth Carlson duly thanked the Zambians and accompanied the officials on a brief tour of the towers while the rest of the athletes returned to their housing at Georgia Tech.

That night, during post-cleaning crew clearance by the guard, those same three well-conditioned human vehicles carefully, and in complete silence, super-glued listening devices onto thirty individual microphones, according to an elaborate color coding system worked out by Harry Thomas, so as to be able to identify the important speakers. The microphones were situated on top of a conference table adjoining the office of the President of Coca Cola. The listening devices were roughly the size of a worn down pencil eraser. Placed in the same place and position on each microphone, they were less noticeable than the direction of the wheels on one of the thirty chairs.

Following that successful venture, they then made the rounds, planting similar devices labeled for various other locations, including the president's office, the president's secretary's office, the four executive vice presidents' offices, the security desk in front of the large oak door in front of the steel vault door, and later, very stealthily, the security desk in the lobby.

As was typical of Coca Cola's amiable president, a large, wide-screened TV had been ordered for the benefit of employees entering or leaving the building, to enable them to catch some of the Olympics. It was during Marvin's very stealthy adventure to the lobby to place the listening device that he also installed the battery powered, remote access controlled camera that would allow Harry to have complete monitoring of the security area. It would be retrieved within twenty-four hours.

All procedures were complete with moments to spare. They retreated into their hideouts, snacking on untrackable, non-crummy snacks from their packs, being sure to keep every ounce of evidence inside the pack. Just before drifting off to catch what sleep they could, each had been instructed to plug in their communication devices, and flick on the power.

Early the following morning, Harry told them that he was about to patch their monitor into the listening devices feed that they had successfully established the night before. Their efforts had worked like a charm!

That night, Bob Arnold was astutely positioned in a spot from outside the towers in which he was able to easily observe the lights in the twentieth floor going off. His assignment was to alert Harry via three dashes and three dots on his own transmitter when the floor went dark.

As soon as he did so, Harry conveyed the message to the three inside, who immediately went to work. They approached the giant, prismed Coke Bottle. Marvin and Gary raised it and held it high enough so that Maggie could slide underneath and attach wheels into the catch holes that had been installed during its creation. Quickly, she performed this task. The three of them confidently rolled it toward the vault. With the prism redirection of light, without effectively interrupting the laser beam mish mash, Gary worked the combination and opened the first vault.

Suddenly, Harry caught a conversation from his lobby listening post that he had not anticipated.

"Control one to unit three."

"Unit three, go ahead control."

"Tony, do me a favor. When you get back to twenty-five, send me down a Diet Coke, some chips and an apple, would ya?"

"Yeah, Frank, but I'm on the media center on twenty-one. Mind if I watch the torch lighting ceremony on the big screen for a couple minutes?"

"Sure. I ain't gonna die from malnutrition in a couple minutes, I guess."

"OK, buddy, I'll see you in a few."

"Unit two to control."

"Go ahead, two."

"Listen, Frank, I'm on seventeen, near the elevators. I'll go up to twenty-five to the snack bar now and then send it down. Then maybe I'll go to twenty-one and catch the ceremony with Tony. OK?"

"Yeah, sure."

Harry was frantic. "Avert!" he screamed into the system, "Avert! Return everything to its original condition!"

The three looked at each other for a stunned second. Then, instantly, they raced to return the Coke Bottle and secured it into its original position, but had no time to remove the wheels. Just then they heard the bell, signaling the arrival of an intruder. Maggie squatted silently inside the bottle, while Marvin ducked into an office on the other side of bottle.

Gary, nearest a sofa, squatted down on the far side. He was in the most critical position, where, if the guard had decided to shine his flashlight, he would most certainly have been spotted. However, he was also in the most advantageous. As the guard walked by, he could make out his shoes going in the direction of the snack bar. A few minutes later, with the three barely breathing for fear of creating noise and giving themselves away, Gary saw the same shoes retreating in the opposite direction. It wasn't until the elevator door opened and closed that they let out their full breaths.

Maggie stood up a minute. Her eyes said it all.

"Now you know why I insisted we get into top shape," Marvin whispered with a smile.

Their second attempt was less nerve-wrecking. Once inside the big vault, inside the protection of the Coke Bottle prism, Maggie was able to reach through a specially designed window and work Mike's victorious combination of the smaller safe. It worked the first time. She extracted the only contents of the small safe—a red case containing the coveted formula. She replaced it with something from her pack, closed the safe and exited smoothly.

Harry had indirectly connected the broadcasting of Bob's guard locations to the three's small earpieces.

"Eighth floor is dark…heading for the seventh…"

The older man's voice was somehow calming as they returned their Trojan Horse to its original position and removed the wheels, returning them to Maggie's pack. As Maggie checked and rechecked for any traces of their presence, Gary and Marvin returned to the conference room with a red case. Marvin took some packing tape from his bag and they taped the case on the underside of the chair situated at the president's spot.

Their task complete, the three exchanged glances of relief. Marvin was accustomed to the process and operating without speaking was not new to him. But it was a more stressful ordeal for the other two than they had imagined. It would be five hours in their hideouts before Harry would deem it safe enough for them to exit.

It was at 4:15 am that Harry gave the order for retreat. At that moment, the security monitors throughout the Coca Cola Towers went to snow for the last time. Gary and Maggie began their descent to the sixth floor, while Marvin dashed all the way down, looked longingly at the lobby level, wishing he could make his exit right then and there. Of course he had only a few seconds remaining. Harry signaled him when he could slide in behind the lobby television, which took some time because the guard had taken a snooze. When he was jostled awake, he strolled down the hall for a cup of coffee.

"Marvin! Go now!"

Marvin shot silently through the corridor, displaced the camera, retraced his steps and returned to the stairwell in under twelve seconds. "I should be in the Olympics," he thought as he began to ascend the stairs, stuffing the camera into his pack.

On the sixth floor, Gary had fastened Maggie's waist security to the pulley system he had designed earlier. "OK," he whispered before giving her a little shove, "you'll be fine."

Maggie gasped at the suddenness of it, but gently landed at the bottom, disengaged herself and sent the pulley back up to Gary for Marvin. Without asking permission, Gary began to attach it to Marvin's waist security.

"Now wait a minute," Marvin began.

Instinctively, Gary told Marvin to hand him his radio. "It'll only weigh you down," he explained.

Gary could hear Harry laughing lightly. "Good one, Gar," he said. "OK, don't let this guy fake you out. He's a tough cookie, he just needs a little assistance sometimes."

"I could probably climb down that gutter rail, there, see it?" Marvin was saying.

"You'll do fine," Gary said.

"Are you ready, Gary?" Harry said.

"Uh huh," Gary responded.

"What did you say? Who are you talking to?" Marvin demanded.

"Go!" Harry said.

With that, Gary gave Marvin a backwards shove, sending the man safely moving down the six-floor distance—but not without shrieks that should have disturbed even the smallest mouse, but didn't.

"I'll get you, Sowell," Marvin said, shaking his fist as he extracted himself from the cable. "But you were right. There wasn't much to it.

Gary's descent was more complex, his needing to be completely outside the building before gliding down. He checked for any dropped items or signs of their presence, then shut the window as planned, attached himself to the outside support cable and took a relatively wide ride down, but ended up hitting the mark anyway.

For comfort and support, the rest of the group were located in various positions around the descent area. After Gary's safe landing, the three casually, but quickly walked down North Avenue, returning to their housing at Georgia Tech.

Chapter Seventeen
Opening Ceremonies

By 6:00 pm that July evening, the housing area for the Olympic athletes, which had come to be known as Olympic Village, was nearly empty. All of the residents had dressed in native costume and were taking their places inside the Olympic Stadium for the Opening Ceremony.

At Crawford Long Hospital, a tall hero with a bruised knee struggled to maintain his composure. A knock came at the door.

"Hey! It's good to see you guys!" Mombasa said, speaking in his native dialect. Eight of his team members had come to pay respects before attending the ceremony. "You look terrific!"

"It's good to see you, Mombasa," Oku, his hometown friend said. "We could not attend this event without first stopping to tell you that you will be missed."

"We wanted you to have your colors," another friend said, laying his costume on the bed, "even if you cannot attend, at least you will be dressed for the event."

Mombasa smiled, his eyes filled with tears. "You are wonderful friends," he said. "I know you will do well. I want you to enjoy the ceremonies tonight."

"We will go with heavy hearts, my friend," said Oku.

"Please—please. Thank you for your considerations," Mombasa objected, "but do not grieve. I am here because of a turn in events. And I am not ashamed of that choice."

The members smiled and bowed their heads. "You are right," said Oku. "We admire you, and will take your spirit with us."

But as they filed out of his room, Mombasa did mourn. Years of training and winning had earned him the chance to compete with the world. And now that he had arrived, he could not participate. It was a bittersweet pill to swallow.

"Whatcha doing?" came a familiar voice from the doorway.

"Hey, Tex!" he said. "When did you get released?"

"I'm not sure," Tex answered, "but the doctor just got around to signing the papers ten minutes ago. What's going on up here? I thought I saw some of your teammates."

"Yes! Yes, they have come to say they'll miss me tonight," Mombasa said.

"Hey, look at that!" Tex said. "You got your Gene Kelly outfit all back in shape. Who did that for you?"

Mombasa laughed. "My Gene Kelly outfit!" he said. "Oku and his buddy did it. They told me I should dress, at least be there in the spirit, as you say."

"That's not a bad idea," Tex said. "You want me to get lost so you can do that?"

"Oh, I don't know. It's very hard to…"

"Hey! Hold on a sec, Mombasa," Tex said, jumping up. He quickly walked down the hall to the nurse's station. "Is Dr. Jarrett on still?" he asked.

"He should be in the building," she said. "I'll check. Are you feeling all right?"

"Oh, yeah, I'm OK," he answered. "But I need to see him pretty urgently about Mombasa."

"What's happened?" the nurse asked, her face instantly registering alarm.

"No, no, it's more psychological," Tex said, trying to sound medical.

"OK," she answered tentatively. "I'll get him to Mombasa's room as soon as I find him."

Tex burst into his buddy's room. "How about getting into the top half of your costume?" he asked. "The doctor will be here soon."

"What's up, Tex?" Mombasa asked, sitting up.

"I've got an idea," was all he said.

The small television in the hospital room showed the diminutive view of the ten thousand plus athletes assembling for the introductory ceremonies. Mombasa, attempting to put on his colorful, official Zambian dress shirt, was heartbroken and curious in equal parts. His curiosity did not last for long.

"So, your partner in heroics has yet another idea to save someone," Dr. Jarrett said heartily as he entered the room, followed by a grinning Tex. Dr. Jarrett bent down to examine Mombasa's knee. "How did you ever get a name like Mombasa when you come from Zambia," he said busily. "Shouldn't you be from Kenya?"

Mombasa grinned. "My mother liked the name," he said. "What is going on? What was your great idea, Tex?"

"Your friend thinks you might be able to *be* at the ceremony if not *participate* in the ceremony," Dr. Jarrett said, standing up. "And I have to say, he's one smart Texan."

"You guys are really unusual," Dr. Jarrett said, shaking his head.

"That's one more thing we have in common," said Mombasa. "Geographical paradoxes."

They laughed.

As a nurse entered, Dr. Jarrett instructed her on the tray he would need to outfit his patient for his journey. He turned to Mombasa. "Son, you're going to need a cast. We call it a walking cast, but I don't want you to take that as any indication that you are to put all your weight on it. I'm giving you a pair of crutches. The injury will heal, but if it is interfered with the injury will not heal as quickly, and it may become more stressed, making it a worse injury overall."

Mombasa lit up. "You will put on a cast that will permit me to attend the Opening Ceremonies?"

"I can't do anything about getting you in over there—I wish I had a ticket—but I can get you into a condition where you can leave the hospital, but on those strict orders I just outlined. Deal?"

"Deal!" Mombasa cried.

Tex made a quick phone call to Harry. "You won't believe this," he said, "but the doc is letting Mombasa out with a walking cast. Can you help us get to the Olympics?"

"I can get you a car there, but if you want to make it in time, you're going to have to keep this thing quiet. The media will hold you up every step of the way."

"Right," said Tex. "I got that."

Within minutes a police car sat patiently at the regular admitting door of the hospital. Such a sight was common and gave no one cause for curiosity. The loan driver sat sipping coffee and occasionally speaking on his radio.

It took a little longer to secure the cast. "It used to be these things had to dry and oh, what a pain it was!" Dr. Jarrett said as he wrapped the knee bracing materials. "Before long, I bet you can buy these things in the drug store. Do-it-yourself knee surgery recovery," he said chuckling.

"I can't fit on my trousers over this," Mombasa said.

"Can you get another pair back home?" Dr. Jarrett asked.

"Sure, I can," said Mombasa.

"OK, well, what we do is we put on the one side, and we cut the other side so it doesn't present a challenge, like so." He stripped open the right pant leg from the lower thigh down. "Now, the nurse will help you get into these. I'll send for a wheelchair. You sign this chart and you're good to go. You're going to have to travel by ambulance."

The journey from Crawford Long to Olympic Stadium was a mere eighteen blocks. But, without Harry's and Marvin's help, the trip would have taken up to an hour. The ambulance driver pulled up behind the police car, waved, and pointed toward Mombasa in the passenger seat, and the policeman jumped into action.

"OK, this is 82A. We're heading out. Watch for me on the right."

As the two vehicles left the hospital parking lot, two additional squad cars appeared out of nowhere, sped ahead of them, lights blinking, sirens blaring, clearing the way. The escorts appeared to enjoy their job, laughing and talking as they closed the distance.

At the entrance to the Olympic Stadium, the police spoke with the gate officials, who opened the gate for the ambulance. A parade had started, in which all of the athletes participated. The delegations were lined up by country, and within each country, teams. The arrangement was alphabetical. As Tex and Mombasa exited the ambulance, their appearance caught the attention of quite a few participants. A runner for the American team, David Owens, caught sight of the famed, wounded Zambian. As the very last country to be represented approached the entry to the stage, David Owens breathlessly pled with the front runners to wait. Owens pointed to the departing ambulance, in front of which stood Tex Jenkins, Mombasa on his shoulders, his cast supported by one of the officers, a huge smile on his face, wearing Tex's cowboy hat.

The crowd in the stadium stood and cheered. At the Yellow Jacket Bar, many dear friends cried tears of joy in front of the television set.

"This has sure been one hell of a day, hasn't it?" Fitz said.

"So far," say a chorus of *F.A.R.T.S.* "Don't get too comfortable."

They all watched as the Zambian flag holders separated from their delegation and marched toward Tex and Mombasa, and then accompanied them back to the team.

Down in front, in the VIP section, the teary eyes of Mrs. Payne, wife of the Olympic Committee President, inspired her to reach for her hanky. Instead of dabbing her eyes, she impulsively waved it high in appreciation, as the crowd continued to cheer Mombasa and Tex. Soon, her companions were doing the same, and within seconds, so was the entire section. As one of the cameras picked up the scene, and broadcast it up on the giant telescreen above, everyone in the stadium fished for tissues or handkerchiefs and waved them in rhythm. As the camera panned the Olympic stands, it showed a gently swaying, sea of white.

Chapter Eighteen
Revelation

Harry had just one more thing to do before retiring for what remained of the night.
Stopping at a payphone near the Varsity, he made a fifty-cent call from a second prepaid card to the home of the Kenneth Carlson.

"Hello?" Carlson answered, clearly unhappy about the early wake-up call.

"Mr. Carlson? I have some important information for you."

"Who is this?"

"That's not important," Harry said. "The thing that matters is that I am in possession of the Coca Cola formula!"

"You've got to be kidding. Who is this!" Carlson shouted.

"No. No, I'm not kidding," Harry said solemnly. "I have the red case with the artwork on the upper left hand corner, reading Coca Cola, and just below it, the name George Woodruff. I'll call you later on today. Goodbye for now."

"Hey! Hold on a minute. Hello. Hello!"

Harry headed for his dorm, careful to switch on the recorders attached to the listening devices installed two nights before in all of the various locations.

It was only 6:00 am when Mr. Carlson arrived in his office. Because of a policy requiring three persons present at the opening of the safe, of either the executive or the board, he had telephoned Wendel Driver, Executive Vice President of Marketing, and Steve Brown, a trusted member of the Board of Directors.

Carlson was widely respected by his associates and employees. He had climbed his way to the top without missing any rungs on the ladder, and for that, he was not resented by anyone. He was a fair man with a respect for everyone, regardless of their position within his company. He visited the homes or sent flowers to the sick and those on staff having operations or giving birth. He went to funerals. But he also showed up at company picnics and softball games, rolling up his sleeves and getting his hands dirty like a regular guy.

Ironically, Carlson had been close to Buzz. Although he never understood why Buzz had turned down opportunity after opportunity to advance within the company, he respected him and openly showed his appreciation.

On that day, his VP and board member arrived nervously. Neither had ever been summoned so early and for such a hush hush meeting as it had been described.

"About an hour ago," Carlson explained to them, "I received a phone call from some clown who said he had possession of the Coca Cola formula. If that's true, then it's not in the vault there. I need you two to witness my opening of it and we'll find out together whether this is an emergency or just some hoax."

Driver and Brown drew themselves up to full height. Carlson went through the series of combinations and at last opened the inside antique safe. When he looked inside, all he saw was an empty can of Pepsi.

"It's true," Carlson said, shutting the safe and closing the vault. "There will be video. There will be documentation of this. Our security system is excellent. You can't beat it."

"But, forgive me for saying so," said Brown, "but before we report anything, I think we'd better give some good hard thought to what such a development will do to the product value, to the dividends—to the stockholders."

"He's right," said Driver. "What would happen if people thought anybody could reproduce the soft drink? It seems to me we'd be in for big trouble."

"I'm not thinking of going to the police," Carlson said. "I am in complete agreement with you gentleman. In fact, I'm not even sure, if at this point in time, the local police would have the manpower to manage anything of this complexity."

"What do you suggest?" Driver asked.

"We'll have it investigated. We'll need a team. This is obviously the work of experienced criminals, and probably more than a few. And they must have inside help—there was no evidence of a disturbance in the laser tracking system whatsoever. What I don't understand is who could it be?"

"Who knows—well, forgive me for asking," Driver said, embarrassed, "but maybe unwittingly someone from the board…"

"It's always the board, isn't it Driver?" Brown said, disgusted. "It could just as easily be a member of the vice presidential squad. How many of you are there, anyway?"

"Gentlemen, gentlemen!" Carlson said, closing his eyes. "No one need make any accusations or even assumptions at this point. I will contact someone I have known and trusted for a long time. Joseph Bretschneider has done work under wraps for IBM, General Electric, and several presidents of the United States. Needless to say, he is a valuable investigator. He's pricy, but he will get results. He'll smoke out any wrong doers without letting the media know he's even working on it. Our relationship has been friendly for some time. We'll arrange a lunch. If anyone recognizes him, which I doubt they will because all eyes are on this Mombasa thing at the moment, we'll just explain that he's here as a guest to enjoy the Olympic Opening. That is if he's available…"

"We can send the jet to get him, can't we?" Brown asked.

"Yes, yes, but that's assuming he's not busy on another assignment," Carlson said.

"What shall we do in the meantime?" Driver asked.

"Keep completely silent about this," Carlson said. "Don't discuss it with your assistants or secretaries—not even your wives, please. There is absolutely no room for loss of discretion. And consider—I don't mean judge—but simply consider who might have had access to either one or both of the vault combinations or any secure information. I can't stress enough—do nothing to investigate or question anyone. Simply use your own brain power to come up with reasonable possibilities."

Carlson rose from the table. "I'll contact you as soon as I have anything further."

"No other members of the board are to be made aware either, at this point?" Brown asked.

"Correct. Only the three of us. Understood?"

The men nodded and rose to exit.

Carlson sighed and headed for his office.

Chapter Nineteen
Wild Goose Chase

Carlson's telephone conversation with Bretschneider provided Harry with details of the private investigator's itinerary—and his companions'. Three investigators would simply be too many to manage. Something would have to be done.

At 6:30 pm, on the night after, as Tex and Mombasa had their day in the Olympic Stadium, Bretschneider received a phone call in his suite at the Marriott Hotel.

"Mr. Bretschneider?" came the young man's voice.

"Yes," Bretschneider answered, not sure what else to say.

"Pleased to speak with you, Bretschneider. It's my understanding that you and your friends are here to investigate a robbery."

"Who is this?"

"Well, the bad guy, of course."

Bretschneider was silent a moment, completely thrown by the thief's admission. "What do you want with me?"

"Actually, it's more a question of what you want with me, isn't it?"

"Look, I don't know who this is…"

"And you're not going to. I'm simply going to offer you the opportunity to assist Mr. Carlson in the presentation of the options he has is a relatively tough situation. Are you game?"

"Absolutely. Where can we meet?"

Harry laughed. "Bretschneider!" he said. "Really. Anyway, what I'm trying to do here is arrange with you an opportunity to discuss options. You'll have to let me know if you're amenable."

"Whatever you say. I'd be grateful."

"OK, here's the ground rules. Number one, I want to talk to only you. And I want you to be by yourself. Clear?"

"Yes, of course."

"Second, I don't want my conversations recorded. That includes this one."

"Fair enough."

"Let's see how it all works out," Harry said. "I want you to meet me tonight. 10:00 at the Marta Station. Go to the bank of pay telephones on the east wall at the rear of Peachtree Center."

"I'll be there."

"Remember our deal, now, all right?"

"Absolutely."

At 8:00 that evening, Bretschneider opened his door to two other gentlemen from out of town.

"It's gonna be a piece of cake," Bretschneider said. "Some idiot. He asks me if I agree not to record his conversation. And to come alone." He began to laugh.

"Oh brother," said Dengler, the younger associate. "But he must have some smarts if he's really got the formula."

"Does he have it, for sure?" asked the other investigator, named Platford. "Carlson got proof?"

"You know, I'm starting to think the thief is the smart guy around here," Bretschneider said. "You think the president of Coca Cola is gonna get us over here in the middle of the day on his private jet to find out if the formula is missing from his safe?"

"OK, so he's sure," said Platford. "You don't have to get so hot about it."

"Let's just get on with the business at hand," Bretschneider said.

"All right, I got the primaries. You gotta raise you shirt. This one ought to be right at about heart level, to pick up the up range. Its set on the mixer already, right about twelve kilohertz."

"What the hell's that supposed to mean?" Bretschneider said.

Dengler cut in. "It gets the high sounds. The other gets other stuff. It really doesn't matter, does it, Platford?"

"Awww, everybody's a critic! OK. Forget the technical talk. Here, take this and stick it—somewhere on your chest."

Bretschneider did so.

"See those tabs?" Platford went on. "They gotta be pushed down, secure 'em good."

"OK," Bretscheider said. "What else?"

After the three had completed the job, they had just about enough time to get to Marta Station by 10:00 pm.

For such a busy night in the city, relatively few people were moving through the station. At the bank of phones, there was a solitary bench. No one sat on it, but a bedraggled woman scuffled around the area, her trembling hands carefully investigating every possible spot for lost change in the pay phones. She wore two different shoes, and a red sweater and heavy slacks. As she rummaged for change in the far phone, it rang.

Bretschneider immediately started for the phone, but never had a chance of being the one to answer it.

"Hello!" the woman's voice burst out. "Hello! Hello!" she screamed at the top of her lungs. "Is anybody home? Hello? Burt Reynolds?"

Bretschneider, unsure how to handle the situation, simply walked forward and backward, and turned around. He gestured to his two associates who sat some distance from him.

"Oh, hello!" cried the woman. "This is Lady Di…Oh, thank you, you sound very nice, too! Would you like to have sex with me?"

"For crying out loud," Bretschneider muttered as he stood near the phone.

"No?" the woman said, surprised. "You're looking for a man. Oh, well, then, you must be a gay one. I can't be bothered with you," and she began to hang up the phone. Suddenly she retracted it. "What? What did you say? I was hanging you up. What did you say?"

Bretschneider sighed heavily.

"Duke Snyder? Isn't that the old fellow? Outfielder, or goalie or something?"

Bretschneider could not hear it, but laughter was bubbling uncontrollably from her earpiece. "Bretschneder!" she said. "Oh, you mean Bretschneider, that's a dog, right?"

"A what? A man? Oh, I see. Let me look around." She set down the phone and peered around her, shading her eyes with her hand. Only feet from her face was the frustrated form of the man in question. When she focused on him, she eyed him up and down suspiciously. "Are you with the circus?" she asked him.

"No…" he answered, unsure how to proceed. "I'm…"

"Are you Bretschneider?" she asked.

"Yes! Yes, that's me! Is the phone call for me?"

"It is. That'll be five dollars. I'll need five dollars for my trouble."

"Here, by all means," Bretschneider said, stuffing the money into her hand. As he took the phone, the woman returned to the business of checking and rechecking the coin return slots for change on the other phones.

When Bretschneider finished his conversation, he went back into the main part of the station, and headed for the southbound train. His two associates were in tow.

When they had left, the woman sat down on the bench. She pulled a cell phone out of her enormous trousers pocket and began to dial. "The subject has taken the southbound train," she said. "His two friends got into the car behind his. How did I do?"

"Fitz, you were an Oscar-winner today for sure—for comedy!" Harry laughed, the tears still rolling down from his eyes.

As Bretschneider sat stiffly in his seat, he looked around himself. He was a good judge of character. Of that fact, he was sure. If the thief was on the train with him, he would know it. Ahead of him, except for one male passenger on the left, cleaning his teeth, the car was empty. Behind him sat an older couple with packages and a single woman.

It's either that clown up ahead of me, he thought to himself, *or possibly the woman. Doubtful though. Both were here when I got on.*

He continued his ride to the airport, where he had been instructed to go in his conversation with Harry. It had been hard to concentrate with the irritating baglady under his elbow, but he knew where to go.

As he departed, the elderly couple lifted their packages and ambled off as well.

"Do you need anything at the smoke shop?" the woman asked as Bretschneider paused.

"Oh, come on, woman," cried the man. "We don't have to stop and shop everywhere we go!"

Bretschneider headed for the security checkpoint. As he passed through, the alarm sounded.

"Please put anything that might activate the alarm in this tray…" began the attendant, but Bretschneider simply peeled off the listening devices from his chest and tossed them into the tray before the man had finished his instruction.

"OK..." began the attendant.

Bretschneider passed through and continued, as he had been directed, meeting up with his other two associates waiting for him at the lower level. Dengler busied himself with a magazine. Platford sat intently, watching females.

At the top of the escalator, the older couple set their packages down and gazed at the scene.

"Well, Charlotte?" said Jack. "Is he a piece of work or what?"

Charlotte laughed. She drew out her cell phone and called Harry. "Subject has passed through security," she said. "He undressed for them, by the way. He's joined the others already. We're heading back."

As the two tossed their bags of newspaper shreds into the trash can, they watched Bretschneider suddenly head for the pay phones.

"This is fun," Jack said, opening the door for Charlotte. "We should have been in on the airport caper."

Bretschneider grabbed the phone quickly, intent on avoiding any repeat performances by comedic bag personnel.

"Hello."

"I'm very disappointed in you," came the voice. "I asked you to be alone—but you have two gentlemen with you! And if that's not enough, you're wired like a Christmas tree."

Bretschneider started to mutter, but was unable to defend himself, and unsure at the same time if it would be a wise thing to try.

Harry would have none of it. "Get on the next shuttle train—all of you. You get off on Concourse A. They stay on the train and get off on Concourse D. They are to go to gate two, where they are to stay put for one hour. Is that clear? If you fail to follow these simple directions, that will be the end of it. There will be no deal. When you get off at

Concourse A, you are to go to the escalator. Ride up. Wait at the pay phones straight ahead."

"OK."

"No more interpretations, Bretschneider."

"OK, OK, I'm going." He signaled to Dengler and Platford that the jig was up. "Come on," he said, disgust in his voice.

The train was nearly there as they ascended the escalator, so they had to rush to make it. Bretschneider was eager to leave his associates behind. "Sit somewheres else," he said to them as they all got on.

He noticed a suspicious looking man as he got on. The man had a tape recorder in his lap. Beside him stood a college-aged couple. The woman had perfect legs that seemed to go on forever. The man gave him a nasty look. When he got ready to get off at Concourse A.

The woman got off ahead. "I'll see ya soon," she said to the man.

Bretschneider headed up the escalator behind her, grateful for the view. The man traveled on to Concourse D, along with Platford and Dengler, where they had no problem complying with instructions, while on payroll to Carlson for $7500 per day.

"Hey, get me a paper," Dengler called as Platford headed for the sundries shop.

"You buy, I'll fly," Platford said, his hand out.

Bretschneider heard the phone ringing. "Yes," he said.

"OK, I want you to go back to the Marta Train—now that you're alone and have left off your wires. And I want you to exit at North Avenue."

"What do I do next?" he asked.

"Pick up the phone at the top of the North Avenue Station. I'll let you know."

As Bretschneider left the set of pay phones, Marta ducked into the ladies room and made her call. "Gary's on the way to D with the other two," she said. "Your guy's on his own."

Bretschneider was not a trim gentleman. The heat and his sudden exertion was creating a certain amount of fatigue. When a businessman with several pieces of luggage sitting on the only bench at the waiting area moved to retrieve it so that he could have a seat, he found himself sincerely grateful.

"Thanks," he said, collapsing onto the bench.

"No problem," said the man. "Can't be taking up the whole bench. Oh! Lookie here. The train's coming."

When they got on the train, they continued their conversation. "You here for the Olympics?" the man asked Bretschneider.

"No, business," Bretschneider answered, exhaling heavily.

"Man! Did you pick the wrong week!"

"You're not kidding!" he said. "It wasn't my idea, I'll tell you that. You here for the games?"

"Nah," the man said. "This is where I live. But I had to take a one-day trip myself, up to New York."

"Oh! This is my stop. This one's North Avenue, right?"

"Yeah, first one."

"Thanks. I'll see ya."

"Good luck!"

Bob smiled. It was quite an adventure.

"Headquarters," he said into his phone. "the subject is headed to the Street. I'm getting off at the next stop. My car is there. I'll see you shortly."

It was at the top of the Marta Station where Detective Bretschneider received his final travel instructions.

"Go west on North Avenue," Harry told him, "past the Varsity to Techwood Drive. Turn right there, and go on the stadium side of the street and enter Gate Eleven.

Among the crowds of people milling around in front of the Varsity was a small group of star seekers, getting an autograph from an American basking in the glory of his fifteen minutes of fame. As Bretschneider passed the Varsity, the American paused to make a phone call.

"Hello, control?" Tex said, "He's just passed me by, headed to Techwood Drive."

"Good work, Tex," Harry said. "I'll see you soon."

As Bretschneider continued his journey up North Avenue and turn right onto Techwood Drive, he passed a police officer at the corner.

"Nice night," he said to the cop.

"Yes, it is," he responded, saluting the passerby. Just then, as Bretschneider made his turn toward Bobby Dodd stadium, he realized that although the facility was darkened, there was some kind of flickering light inside.

"Hello!" he called in a loud whisper.

"Sir," a voice said very politely from behind him, "please sit in the chair there between the two candles to your right."

Bretschneider sat, looking around him, but in the odd light of the candle, seeing nothing but darkness.

"I'm sure you'll appreciate the fact that I need you to remain seated in that direction," the voice said.

The detective recognized the voice. It was the very same one whom he'd spoken with earlier that day, and on all of the various telephones over the preceding hour.

"I'm not gonna turn around," he said.

"Mr. Bretschneider, I appreciate your help in this matter. I know it's been difficult this evening, but I'm sure you can sympathize, well perhaps that's a poor choice of words. At least you can understand my need to divert your position several times."

"Look, I'm just trying to get some information," Bretschneider said. "That's all."

"Of course," Harry went on. "My demands are simple. As it stands, Coca Cola has three options: Number One, Carlson can do nothing and I will sell the formula to the highest bidder; Number Two, I receive fifteen million dollars in cash in exchange for the return of the formula; or Number Three, Coca Cola buys that tall building there to your left from the city for that same sum, fifteen million dollars. That building is called Roosevelt Towers. It represents a senior citizen housing facility. As the new owners, Coca Cola keeps the building as it is, a place for senior citizens to continue residing as they have done for dozens of years. I'm sure that as a businessman yourself, you would certainly see that the exchange of something for something is a far better choice than something for nothing, as in option two, and makes even more sense than option one, which would be catastrophic for the company."

"I'll deliver the message," Bretschneider said. "But what's all this to you? What do you care about all those people?"

"My goal in meeting with you tonight is to ensure that the message be delivered to Coca Cola," Harry said.

"I understand," Bretschneider said. "Are you an envoy for someone else?"

"Mr. Bretschneider," Harry said. "Why don't you just ask me my name and how it's spelled?"

"I'm sorry," said Bretschneider. "I guess that was a stupid move."

"Let's just put it this way," Harry said, creating as he went along. "I was a student years ago at Georgia Tech. I used to study there in that little park across the street from the Coca Cola Towers. I'd spend my time daydreaming, wondering all sorts of things—would it one day be possible for me to have that most valuable piece of information—that incredible recipe that set apart Coca Cola from so many others, making them millions and millions every year? But don't get me wrong. It wasn't about the money. It was the challenge that intrigued me. I guess it was engineer in me—how could it be done? To put their minds at ease, feel free to tell Carlson that I've had the formula in my possession for over five years. I've never shown it to a soul. I never even told anyone about it. But then, this past spring, I read an article in the newspaper about the Roosevelt Towers, and how all of its residents, who are all seniors, were to be relocated like so many cattle because the city had decided it would be more profitable to sell their building than to maintain it. I guess you could say, especially in the wake of one death already due to the impact of this news, that this is my way of trying to show a little community spirit."

Harry took a deep breath. He was more involved in the situation than he had expected to be. "I will call you tomorrow at Carlson's office at 1:30 for their answer," he said. "Good night, and thank you."

Bretschneider rose, and slowly turned toward the exit. As he walked away, toward the lights of Techwood Avenue, he heard the gate clunk closed behind him. He turned, but saw nothing.

He was headed to the Varsity next. He had a presentation to make the next day, and he would need a little time to think the thing out.

Chapter Twenty
Coke's Decision

"Gentlemen," Mr. Carlson said to Brown and Driver, "This is Joseph Bretschneider. Mr. Bretschneider is the man I told you about. He's got some information for us this morning and I'd like you to pay careful attention and give me your feedback.

Bretschneider was moderately ill at ease absent his bumbling associates. As excellent of a team as they were, they were the clumsy ones. Their presences always made him feel superior, and confident.

"Well, Mr. Carlson, Brown, Driver," he said, "it seems I have been in contact with the thief—or thieves—although I believe this to be the work of one man." He cleared his throat and puffed up his chest to begin his long speech. "In my estimation the perpetrator, although devious, is not a bad person…"

"Mr. Bretschneider," Driver interrupted, "did he say he had the formula?"

"Er, well, I was getting to that."

"I think we should move along the most direct lines," Carlson said. "A profile on the person or persons in question can always be of great value following the return of the goods, but for the moment, I think what we are most interested in is the whereabouts of our formula." He smiled gently, a shade above patronizingly.

"Of course," Bretschneider said. "I'll be brief. Essentially, the thief has outlined three options for the return of the Coca Cola formula. I will make any recommendations you like after I have completed his options."

The three men listened to Bretschneider relate the information with increasing interest. When he had finished, Carlson exchanged glances with Brown and Driver.

"So," he began, "this is a bit of a crusade? Something along those lines?"

"Apparently," Bretschneider answered. "I couldn't swear that he's sincere, but he seems to have laid out the groundwork for achieving exactly what he indicates that he wants."

Carlson was thoughtful. "Thank you, Bretschneider," he said sincerely, "we need to discuss this."

Bretschneider rose. "I understand your need for privacy," he said, "but I should tell you that the thief has requested that I be here at 1:30 to give your answer."

"That's good," Carlson said, rising and shaking his hand. "Let's say we meet back here in two hours. About 12:30?"

"Fine." Bretschneider left, relieved.

Back at headquarters, Harry took off his headphones and smiled. He stepped over to the coffee machine to get himself a fresh cup. Things were going well so far. When he started listening again, Carlson was already in conversation with the other two.

"...and that's what I'm saying," Carlson said. "This must remain a matter between the three of us and Bretschnieder's team. However, we can certainly get input from the other departments and members of the board. This is an opportunity that may actually have some positive repercussions. I'd like to get some input on what they might be. I'd like the two of you to meet me back here in an hour. We'll have lunch sent in. Driver, speak with all of the VPs. Get their take on this. Brown, I want you to talk to at least another board member or two. As President and Chairman, I don't need board approval to make this purchase, but I would like input nevertheless."

At 11:30, a tray was wheeled into the president's office. On it sat three large salads and a plate of sandwiches, glasses of ice, a bowl of fresh fruit, a pitcher of iced tea, and a tray of desserts.

"Put it over there," Carlson's assistant directed. "And please bring up coffee service as well."

After everything was set up, the assistant withdrew and closed the doors. Just then, Carlson appeared. "Lunch ready?" he asked.

"Yes, sir. It's in there now. Coffee's just been brought up, too."

"Excellent. Thank you, Claire," Carlson said smiling. "Have a nice lunch yourself. We'll be busy most of the afternoon, so please don't forward any calls."

"Yes, sir, thank you, sir," Claire said, taking her seat.

Driver and Brown both appeared at that point, and all three bustled into Carlson's office and closed the door.

"Please help yourselves to lunch," Carlson said. "We'll sit at the conference table here. But let's talk as we eat. I'd like to have a good handle on what you have to tell me before Bretschneider returns."

"I'll start, if you like," said Brown. "Charlie Haines has been concerned about our tax liability this year. The business from these games has been phenomenal, as expected. But he knew nothing had been done to offset that in the tax department. He felt the idea would be excellent, provided it could be accomplished before the end of the third quarter."

"That bodes well with the accounting department," Driver cut in. "That was exactly the message I got from Blackmon."

"OK," Carlson said, "did you talk to anyone else?"

"Yes, I had a few words with my deputy in marketing. He agrees that it would provide us an excellent natural backdrop to televised football games; the roof of Roosevelt Towers can be Coca Cola's answer to the least expensive blimp in the history of advertising. Our signs would be visible not only to the public and attendees, but to the television audiences nationwide. The sign would be programmed differently for every game or season. Additionally, Roosevelt Towers is highly visible to downtowners. Additional neon could be added to the face of the building."

Carlson was pleasantly surprised by the idea. "Excellent, Driver," he said, shaking his head. "Excellent idea! Anything else?"

Brown and Driver both had had time to discuss the idea from a public relations perspective.

"Thirty-five percent of our stock is held by senior members and shareholders," Brown said. "It wasn't much of a surprise to hear their thoughts on it."

"The two are connected. There's no way to get bad publicity for purchasing a retirement apartment house and leaving it in tact," Driver said. "I just hope it's not more expense than benefit."

Brown struggled to defeat an instinct to condescend. "Of course the benefits outweigh the possible expense!" he said. "If Coca Cola is suddenly seen as the beverage of choice for the sixty-five and older group—we've got it made! Even if we pay one million dollars a year to maintain—if we have to *rebuild* the damn building—we're way ahead."

Carlson nodded. "I see your point," he said. "I think we have a decision. Let's get Bretschneider in here."

Seconds later, the private line rang. Bretschneider hastened through the door to answer it, bumping his rear carriage against a hollow filing cabinet, which reverberated harshly into the phone. Harry lifted his headphones, grimacing.

"Hello?" Bretschneider said. "Hello?"

Within a few seconds, Harry stopped seeing stars, and returned the headphones to his ears.

"Hello!" Bretschneider called, eyeing Carlson with concern.

"Yes! Yes…Hello," said Harry, jumping a second time. "I'd like to speak to Bretschneider, please."

"This is Bretschneider."

"Fine. Has your client reached a decision regarding our conversation?"

"Uh…"

He covered the phone with his hand. "Have you reached a decision? He wants to know."

"Tell him we'll buy the Towers," Carlson said.

"Coke will buy Roosevelt Towers," Bretscheider said.

There was a moment of silence on the other end, during which Harry struggled with a sudden, unexpected deluge of emotion.

"Hello?" Bretschneider said. "Are you there?"

"Yes," Harry continued. "Thank you."

"Uh…"

"Ask Mr. Brown to select a number between one hundred fifteen and two hundred eleven."

Bretschneider scratched his head. "I wish this was on a speaker phone," he said to Carlson. "This guy wants Mr. Brown to pick a number between one hundred fifteen and two hundred eleven."

Carlson smiled slightly and shrugged. "Go ahead, Brown."

"I'll take one hundred sixty-five," Brown answered.

"He says one hundred sixty-five," Bretschneider related.

"OK, now ask Driver to choose a number between one and four."

Bretschneider looked at Driver. "Your turn. Choose between one and four."

"Two," Driver said, looking confusedly at Carlson.

Carlson simply shrugged, apparently amused at the antics of the thief.

"He said two," Bretschneider said.

"Thank you," Harry continued. "OK, now ask Mr. Carlson to select a number between one and forty-five."

"It's your turn, sir," Bretschneider said, turning to Carlson. "He wants you to choose a number between one and forty-five."

"OK," Carlson said almost cheerfully, "how about twenty-three?"

"Twenty-three," Bretschneider repeated.

"Thank you," Harry said. "Will you please get out the current issue of the Atlanta Yellow Pages and turn to page one sixty-five?"

Bretschneider did so. "Now what?"

The other three men were clearly intrigued by the process.

"Please go to column number two on that page, and count down to the twenty-third name."

"All right," Bretschneider said after some time.

"What do you have?"

"It says 'The Law Firm of Kennicott and Wright.'"

"The next thing you need to do is to have whichever of those two partners specializes in real estate present in this office tomorrow morning at 10:00 am. Got that?"

"Yes, tomorrow 10:00 am with the real estate partner at Kennicott and Wright."

"Thank you. Have a nice day."

Carlson looked at Bretschneider as he hung up. "What did he say?"

"He seems pleased," Bretschneider said.

"He's a flake," said Driver.

"Gentlemen," Carlson said, "I'd like to hear what the man had to say. There's something unusual about this character. I'm starting to wonder if it's someone I know."

"If so, you'll never know," Bretschneider said. "You can bet every single call was made with an untraceable credit card, every step..."

"No, that's not my concern," Carlson said, shaking his head. "I am speaking metaphorically. Go ahead, Bretschneider, tell me what he said."

"He said to have either Kennicott or Wright of the Kennicott and Wright Firm in this listing," he tapped the Yellow Pages, "that is the real estate partner here, tomorrow, at 10:00 am. I guess he wants to make sure this happens."

"He didn't ask for ransom, anything additional for himself?" Carlson asked.

"No."

Carlson looked thoughtful. "All right. That's that for now. Look sharp, gentlemen! It's not the end of the world. This is a good thing, I think. Bretschneider, please see that the appropriate real estate attorney is here tomorrow, and we'll all recommence at 10:00 am."

"Sir," Bretschneider began, "regarding my next move..."

"Hold off on anything further," Carlson said, cutting him off. "Let's just take this one step at a time."

"We will lose time, though," Bretschneider insisted.

"And it won't come out of your salary," Carlson assured him. "I appreciate your concerns, and your professionalism. We'll all meet back here at 10:00 am, until then—I've got some games to see!"

The next morning, right at 10:00, the very same phone rang. Bretschneider answered.

"Hello," said the voice. "May I speak with Mr. Kennicott or Mr. Wright?"

"Mr. Douglas Wright is present," Bretschneider said. "I'll hand you over to him."

"Please put us on speaker phone," he said. After a moment, Harry continued. "Hello, Mr. Wright. Do you know anyone in the room?"

Mr. Wright looked perplexed. "Well…not personally," he answered.

Harry continued. "The Coca Cola Company would like to make the purchase of the Roosevelt Towers, a senior citizens residence located at North Avenue and Techwood Drive. The city has advertised the property for sale at a purchase price of fifteen million dollars. We wish to avoid any pricing wars by settling the matter quickly and on a cash basis. Therefore, Mr. Carlson would like to make the offer directly to the city's mayor, Mayor Campbell by 12 noon.

"In the event that you have not caught it on the news, the property has already been approved for sale by the city council. Please set the wheels in motion, and seal the deal with a press conference announcement set for twelve noon tomorrow. The Coca Cola Company will transfer the full amount of fifteen million dollars to your escrow account tomorrow morning by 9:00 am. You will handle the details, the transfer of title, any necessary paperwork resulting from this rapid transaction.

"You will also be available at tomorrow's noonday news conference to answer any questions. Until then, this is to be kept confidential on a need-to-know basis only. For your services and expenses during the next twenty-six to twenty-seven hours, your fee will be twenty-five thousand dollars. I hope this amount is acceptable. Mr. Carlson will have your check ready for you when you leave this morning."

Mr. Wright exhaled and nodded at the same time, as if he'd just been hit in the face with a frying pan, but liked the flavor of what was cooking. "OK," he said tentatively. "I think I understand what you want."

"Thank you for your help, Mr. Wright. Will you please leave the room now? I need to discuss something in private with the other gentlemen."

He looked at Carlson for approval, who nodded.

"Yes, of course. Gentlemen, I'll be in the reception area if you should need me."

"That's fine," said Carlson.

"He's left," said Bretschneider. "Do you want to stay on speaker phone?"

"Fine, thank you," Harry responded. "One hour after the news conference, announcing your purchase and intentions to maintain the senior residences as they are, your formula will be returned. For your information, the seal on the case was never broken. No one has seen the formula."

Mr. Carlson sighed and leaned back in his chair. The other two watched him.

"I must also ask that this remain a secret," Harry continued, "that you do not continue this investigation."

Bretschneider looked at Carlson, who nodded.

"Of course, I can only make that a request. I appreciate your cooperation in this matter."

Then the phone was hung up, in a gentlemanly fashion.

Chapter Twenty-One
Endings...

The following day at twelve o'clock noon, in the Coca Cola Company's auditorium, Mayor Bill Campbell, Carlson, Driver, Brown, and a very quenched but satisfied looking Douglas Wright sat in the lights, flashes, and heat of a hastily arranged news conference. The mayor took the opportunity to improve his image with the senior citizen population by making the announcement himself.

"It gives me great pleasure this morning to announce to the people of Atlanta that the Coca Cola Bottling Company has moved to make the purchase of the recently made available Roosevelt Towers, the senior citizens residence, located at North Avenue and Techwood Drive. As it was announced previously, the purchase price to the city was fifteen million dollars. Although the city might have stood to make a greater profit on another deal, the council and I have accepted the offer made by the Coca Cola Bottling Company due to the stipulation that the Roosevelt Towers will remain as it has been for the last twenty years, a senior citizens home, housing the many and valuable human beings that make our fine city great and prosperous."

The mayor paused for the applause by some of the local residents.

"Thank you," he said, nodding his head in appreciation for all he had done for the senior residents. "Yes, we do value our seniors in Atlanta."

The press conference was mercifully brief, and by 12:30, the participants headed to their respective offices.

At 1:00 pm, the telephone rang in Carlson's conference room, where he, Driver, Brown, and Bretschneider had assembled. Bretschneider had grown accustomed to answering the phone for Carlson.

"Hello."

"Hello. Thank you for the show. It was quite enjoyable. Would you please put me on the speaker phone again?"

He signaled to Brown for help on switching to speaker phone. "OK, they're switching it now," Bretschneider said. "Go ahead."

"Thank you. I will need the assistance of the two gentlemen, now."

"I believe you said that the formula would be returned by now," Bretschneider cut in.

"If you would allow me to continue," Harry said, stifling a laugh, "I was about to ask for the assistance of Messers Brown and Driver."

"OK," said Brown, "we're here."

"Will you two gentlemen be so kind as to turn Mr. Carlson's chair upside down?"

Carlson knew it just then. He began to smirk.

Bretschneider looked at him as though he'd gone crazy. "Just do it, guys," he said.

The two struggled to raise the heavy chair and turned it upside down. Their eyes grew wide. They looked at Carlson, who burst into open, easy laughter. There lay the red case, fully intact, taped to the bottom of the chair. As promised, its seal had never been broken.

As the room grew with laughter and expressions of relief, Harry quietly hung up.

As he did so, the room in which he sat burst with excitement and deeply felt joy. Twelve celebrating seniors and students, and one imported honorary *F.A.R.T.S.* from Africa, sang the praises of Harry, each other, and man's basic goodness. Somewhere in the mix, an odd trombone and clarinet duet could be heard, playing "Happy Days Are Here Again."

Before dark fell that very day, a helicopter crew had raised a sign rushed through production, reading: Coca Cola Takes Hats Off to Seniors! It depicted a group of three, tossing Olympic hats in the air, and holding Cokes. The debacle of its placement drew rapt attention from the crowd already assembled to watch the continuing Olympic Games. Television crews from all networks covered the event, sending it back to national and international affiliate stations.
By close of business that day, the New York Stock Exchange registered an unprecedented single-day twenty-point gain on Coca Cola stock.

Somehow, via computer wizardry that Mike couldn't explain, Morton's Steakhouse in downtown Atlanta had a 9:00 pm reservation for twelve in the name of Mr. Harry Thomas. It was a popular spot that night. As the twelve trickled in early, to enjoy Buzz's birth bath in and out martinis, in honor of the friend who couldn't join them, three tired but happy detectives sat across the room. The coincidence was no coincidence.

"I gotta tell you," Platford was saying, "after twenty-two years with the FBI, and fifteen years in private service, this has got to be the first time I've ever been *happy* that we didn't get our man."

"I think we'll all take a little bit of happiness from a fifty thousand dollar bonus!" Dengler said, raising his glass.

"Hey, it wasn't our assignment to get the guy—it was just to get back the formula. So we did what we were told. And don't you worry about that fifty grand. It ain't gonna cut in on Carlson too much. Did you catch that twenty-point rise in stock this afternoon?"

"Oh yeah," Platford said. "The major stockholder there's gotta be worth at least a hundred million more tonight."

"You know, I got a call from him this evening," Bretschneider went on. "He's gonna need us again. A little less exciting but no less lucrative. Seems he's got the idea that it might not be a bad idea to check out the feasibility of doing a senior citizen complex in Tallahassee, next to Florida State University."

"That's his alma mater," Dengler said. "Makes sense." Just then, the waiter stopped at their table. "Here you are gentlemen, compliments of the large party at the bar, there."

"Who the hell knows us in Atlanta?" Bretschneider said.

The waiter handed him the bar phone.

"Thanks again," came the familiar voice. "Have yourselves a safe trip back home to Philadelphia."

As Bretschneider and the group looked over to their benefactors across the room, they caught sight of Harry just hanging up the phone. The *F.A.R.T.S.* and *ettes* raised their glasses. Maggie tossed her head and thrust her figure forward with a coquettish grin, while Marvin saluted mock seriously in a policeman like fashion. Fitz waved the five-dollar-bill she'd suckered Bretschneider out of, and Mike held up his computer printed graphic of Coca Cola. The rest just laughed and waved.

The detectives raised their glasses in response and shook their heads in amazement.

"Shit," said Platford.

The party of twelve enjoyed their celebratory dinner more than anything since the loss of Buzz. In the spirit of continuing their celebration, Harry asked the waiter to put together a take-out selection of all of the restaurant's assortment of desserts, coffee, and finest cigars.

"How about a farewell to this caper at the 'Up There'?" he asked, to which everyone responded favorably.

The night was clear and beautiful. With the bustle of activity all around them, the imminent departure of the five younger members of the group was somehow less sorrowful. It was agreed that a reunion would take place in four years—exactly Opening Day of the Summer Olympics in Sydney, Australia in the year 2000.

"Let's see how fast you all can get through the airport that time," challenged Fitz.

"It won't be the same without Charles Cronin's help," Harry said. "But it'll be a welcome challenge, right Mike?"

"Oh yeah, don't you worry," Mike said. "We'll make it!"

Epilogue

At the 2000 games, all of the members would show, and these are a few things they were to learn about each other:

Harry Thomas and Maggie Hackett were married and had already produced two offspring. Harry heads up the Atlanta detective office for Bretschneider;

Marta Rives accepted a position as assistant girls' basketball coach at Georgia Tech for two years, and is now head coach for West Chester University in West Chester, Pennsylvania;

Gary Sowell has pursued his dream and become a special rides designer for Six Flags Adventure Parks. He has achieved acclaim within the industry for his "Great Escape Slide," a ride based on a system of supports and pulleys;

Mike Nixon went into business for himself designing computer safety systems;

Bob Arnold and Charlotte Gaffney have become "an item" but do not plan to marry—such a move would call for surrender of one of their social security checks. They are avid runners, and travel all of Charlottes regular haunts together. They entered the 2000 Peachtree Road Race and out of fifty thousand participants finished thirty-eight thousand, three hundred sixtieth and thirty-eight thousand, three hundred sixty-first. The women on Bob's floor marvel at Charlotte's stamina;

Dave Schwelfer did win the Big Game Jackpot to the tune of fifty million dollars. He finagled a deal with Coke to purchase the Roosevelt Towers, a move which somehow served to boost stocks even higher, and also invested in his own beer company, which he named "Buzz Beer;"

Marvin Lemons has taken up skydiving. During football season, he skydives into Bobby Dodd Stadium to start the home games. He dresses in a yellow jacket outfit, and stimulates a student body buzz from the jump from the plane to the landing on solid ground. The rest of the year, he is simply known as the "Flying Lemon," patron to all victims of rogue car dealers. If the dealer fails to right his wrong, the Flying Lemon will descend upon him in a rain of publicity, from a plane;

Jack McBride, not surprisingly, became a valued asset and assistant football coach at Georgia Tech. He is already in heaven;

Tex Jenkins and Mombasa joined forces and developed an import-export business, the primary product being cowboy hats exporting to Africa;

Fitz spends part of her time at the beloved farm in Woodstock, Georgia that was willed to her by her parents. She reportedly has once again christened that special loft in the barn; and

Mombasa, who took the gold that year, and once again in 2000, is shooting for his third consecutive Olympic Gold Medal in the 2004 Olympics.

...Look for other novels by Brendan Brogan coming soon!

* **Edisto**—scheduled for release in Fall, 2003; and
* **Horsebridge**—schedule for release in early Winter of 2003.

EASTON ONE PRODUCTIONS
Publishing Fine Works across the USA

---

131 Eighth Street, South
Brigantine, NJ 08203
Email: ccwords@aol.com